HAMISH HAMILTON

Published by the Penguin Group

Penguin Books Ltd, 80 Strand, London WC2R 0RL, England

Penguin Group (USA) Inc., 375 Hudson Street, New York, New York 10014, USA

Penguin Group (Canada), 90 Eglinton Avenue East, Suite 700, Toronto, Ontario, Canada M4P 2Y3
(a division of Pearson Penguin Canada Inc.)

Penguin Ireland, 25 St Stephen's Green, Dublin 2, Ireland (a division of Penguin Books Ltd)

Penguin Group (Australia), 250 Camberwell Road, Camberwell, Victoria 3124, Australia
(a division of Pearson Australia Group Pty Ltd)

Penguin Books India Pvt Ltd, 11 Community Centre, Panchsheel Park, New Delhi – 110 017, India

Penguin Group (NZ), 67 Apollo Drive, Mairangi Bay, Auckland 1310, New Zealand
(a division of Pearson New Zealand Ltd)

Penguin Books (South Africa) (Pty) Ltd, 24 Sturdee Avenue, Rosebank, Johannesburg 2196, South Africa

Penguin Books Ltd, Registered Offices: 80 Strand, London WC2R 0RL, England

www.penguin.com

First published in the United States of America by McSweeney's 2007
First published in Great Britain by Hamish Hamilton 2007

1

The moral right of the author has been asserted

Printed in Singapore

A CIP catalogue record for this book is available from the British Library

ISBN-13: 978-0-241-14391-9

© 2007 McSweeney's Quarterly Concern, San Francisco, California. It's December 15, 2006 as we write this, which means that the office is filled with three feet of real snow brought in by tanker truck from the high Sierras. A couple of weeks ago we received this note: "I am currently editor-at-large and fiction editor for *The* [redacted] *Goat*, the University of the [redacted] undergraduate literary magazine here in Sewanee, [redacted]. An unpleasant question of staff-member integrity has arisen in the past month. A new staff member, [redacted], informed me as editor-at-large that he had been published in *McSweeney's*, which was part of my reasoning for extending him a personal invitation to join the literary-magazine staff. However, his behavior and overall attitude have led me to question whether or not he was indeed telling me the truth. Already, he most likely will be asked to leave *The Mountain* [redacted] staff due to his lack of professionalism and tact, but I would like to clarify whether or not your publication actually did accept and publish his work." Suffice it to say, this redacted dude had not appeared within these pages. And while we cannot condone using our scrawny name in vain, it nevertheless made us uncomfortable to imagine this resolute editor-at-large brandishing our response at a makeshift hearing in a Sewanee coffeeshop, maybe slamming down a printout of our correspondence in front of her perhaps tactless but still conceivably decent colleague, so we more or less avoided her question. In general, it's our policy to allow all American undergraduates to claim publication in our journal for the purpose of eliciting personal invitations to membership from Tennessean editors-at-large, but this could be a mistake. ¶This issue was actually finished just after Issue 21, which was finished after Issue 22. For a while there, because of printing intricacies, our production lineup bent back on itself like that, but now we've straightened it out and as a company, we have 2007 pretty much settled in our heads: three more quarterlies of indeterminate form, several catergory-shattering projects, and two novels. One of the novels is *Arkansas,* by John Brandon, who drive a windshield-delivery truck in Virginia and writes sentences like this all day long: "He was the kind of kid who'd never worn sandals or a scarf. All kids had begun to look about thirteen to Joyce, except this one." Those two aren't even from the book, so we're not spoiling anything. But you can see, even from these, how good this novel will be. The other novel is a debut by an eighty-nine-year-old named Millard Kaufman. He was nominated for an Oscar in 1956 (screenwriting, *Bad Day at Black Rock*) and tells punchy stories about Billy Wilder and fighting in WWII (Marines, Guadalcanal). He's a terrific man, and his book—called for now *Appointment in Coproliabad,* or maybe *The Secret Formula of the Shit Bricks*—is a terrific one, rollicking and resonant and wordy. It reminds us of Roth and Bellow and Saunders and lots of other writers who know how to splatter the page with life. This is how it begins: "If you look closely at a detailed map of Iraq, you'll find somewhere to the south, between the western shelf and the equally monotonous eastern plain, the province of Assama, a flat depression in the shape of a chicken." ¶Other things that will appear or occur in 2007: a new 826 tutoring center will open its doors in Boston; the *Believer* will release its fiftieth issue; some architecture students will try to build a loft in our office. It's now our ninth year of this enterprise; by 2014, McSweeney's will function much like an animated Jazz Age production line, with vigorous spigots distended by and then expelling innovative literature into milk bottles you'll get on your doorstep every day at 5 a.m., delivered by bouncing sentient trucks. Until then, it's an ad-hoc operation, and you make it and us possible. INTERNS: Kerry Folan, Maxwell Klinger, Rhodes Yepsen, Mattie Bamman, Lauren Hall. COPY EDITOR: Caitlin Van Dusen. EDITORS-AT-LARGE: Gabe Hudson, Lawrence Weschler, Sean Wilsey. WEBSITE: John Warner w/ Ed Page. OUTREACH: Angela Petrella. CIRCULATION: Heidi Meredith. ASSOCIATE EDITOR: Jordan Bass. MANAGING EDITOR: Eli Horowitz. PRESIDENT: Barb Bersche. EDITOR: Dave Eggers.

Outer jacket and interior illustrations: Andrea Dezsö. Inner jacket designed by Brian McMullen and Dave Eggers with text, drawings, and concept by Dave Eggers.

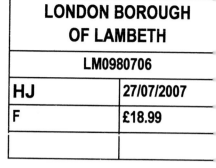

WELLS TOWER

RETREAT

I HAD NOT SPOKEN to my brother Matthew in thirteen months when he telephoned me last autumn.

"Hey there, buddy. Ask you a question. What's your thinking on mountains?"

"I have no objection to them," I told him.

"Good, good," he said. "Did you hear I bought one? I'm on top of it right now."

"Which one? Is it Popocatepetl?"

"Hey, go piss up a rope." The mountain didn't have a name, as far as he knew. He said it was in the north of Maine, which is where he'd been living since July. Wind was blowing into the phone.

"You didn't move again."

"Oh, yes I did," said Matthew. You could hear he was talking through a grin. "I'm gone, little man. Must have been certifiable to stay in Myrtle Beach so long."

Maine sounded nice, I told him. Could he see the ocean from where he was?

"Hell no, I'm not on the *coast*," he roared. "I'm through with coasts. Didn't move twelve hundred miles just to come up here and bark my shins on a bunch of Winnebago people in lobster bibs."

Then his tone softened and he told me that the winter was coming, and that he'd like to see my face before the snows sealed him off from the world.

I said I probably couldn't spare the time, and Matthew began to emit an oral brochure of the property's virtues, its bubbling brooks, forests, and glassy ponds, and the "bold, above-canopy views" from his cabin on the summit, which he described to the last nailhead and bead of caulk. "And I got a guy out here with me who's your type of man. My buddy Bob, my neighbor. I've got him working on the crib. Outstanding guy. Mathematical opposite of those douchebags down in Myrtle. You guys could talk some good shit together. Let me put him on."

I tried to protest, but Matthew had taken his ear from the phone. The sound of a banging hammer rose in the receiver. Then the banging stopped, and a thin, chalky voice came on the line. "Yup, Bob Brown here. Who'm I talking to?"

"This is Alan—"

"Not Alan Dupree?"

"No. I'm Matthew's brother. I'm Alan Lattimore."

"Well, I can believe that over Alan Dupree. Good to know you."

The hammering started up again, and Matthew came back on the line.

"That's the wild man for you," Matthew said with a kind of chuckling pride. "Just him and me—pretty much a two-dude nation is what we've got out here. You'd go bananas for it. When can we put you on a plane?"

It was hard not to share Matthew's pleasure at his departure from Myrtle Beach. The world he'd inhabited there was every bit as worth fleeing as a Vietnamese punji trap—a shadowless realm of salt-scalded putting greens, of russet real-estate queens with sprawling cleavages pebbled up like brainfruit hide, of real-estate men with white-fleeced calves, soft bellies, and hard, lightless eyes, men who called you "buddy-ro" as they talked up the investment value of condominiums already tilting into the Atlantic.

I would have applauded Matthew more heartily for abandoning his life down there had he not already insisted, over the years, that I applaud him for dropping out of law school at Emory, for quitting a brokerage in Memphis, for pulling out of a venture-capital firm he'd launched in Fort Lauderdale, for divorcing his first wife (a quiet, freckled woman I'd liked very much) on the grounds, as he put it to me, that she was "hard of hearing and her pussy stank," and for engaging himself to Kimberly Oosten, Esq., the daughter of an Oldsmobile dealer in Myrtle Beach.

You could trace Matthew's rotations to his early days at school. He'd been an awkward boy, eager to be liked, with eyes as large and guileless as a mule's. He spent his school years chasing acceptance to one social set or another—gerbil enthusiasts, comic-book collectors, the junior birders, the golf club, the hot-rod men, et cetera, without much success. He had a way of coming off as both fawning and belligerent. He was routinely ridiculed and occasionally beaten up by the boys whose friendship he most ardently pursued. His discarded careers notwithstanding, Matthew, at age forty, had accumulated a good amount of money, and I imagine could have bought himself permanent membership in whatever society he liked. But it seemed to me that years ago, this had stopped being the point. Somehow, he'd gotten to a place where he wasn't happy if he didn't pause every four or five years and abort the life he'd had before. After a few years of living comfortably in a place, he would grow restless and hostile, as though he suspected he was being deliberately swindled out of the better life owed to him someplace else.

I live in Arcata, California, where I earn a slim livelihood as a music therapist, an occupation of so little consequence in my brother's eyes that he can never seem to remember exactly what it is that I do for a living. Though I did not have spare time or money to squander on a trip to Maine, as Matthew's pitch wore on I found it heartening that he had once again called me, the sole emissary from his past, to preside over his latest metamorphosis, and in the end I booked a ticket.

I left the first Thursday in November, along a cheap and brutal route. I flew out of Arcata midday to the San Francisco airport, where I spent four listless hours in the company of a man with a wristwatch the size of a plaster ceiling medallion. He tugged ceaselessly at the thighs of his trousers, currying the spare fabric into a blousy pavilion at his crotch. "Edward is really riding roughshod when it comes to our intentionality" is a sentence I heard him utter in two different conversations on his cellular phone. I caught the overnight flight from San Francisco to Boston, hunkered in the lee of an enormous woman whose bodily upholstery entirely swallowed our mutual armrest. I had no place to rest my head. She saw me eyeing the cushioned cavern formed by her shoulder and wattle, and she said, "Go on, stick it right in there." I did so. The woman gave off a clean, comforting aroma of the sea, and I slept very well.

From Boston, I caught a dawn flight to Bangor. In Bangor, I was ushered onto a tiny six-seater that sat on the tarmac for two hours while a mechanic who did not look fifteen peered learnedly at the wing. At last, the engines cranked, and the plane lifted in quavering flight for northern Aroostook County.

Unimaginable vastnesses of spruce and pine forests passed beneath the plane, unbroken by town or village. We landed at an airport that was little more than a gravel landing strip with a Quonset hut off to one side. A solid chill was on the air. The four people I'd flown in with grabbed their luggage from where an attendant had strewn it on the blue gravel, and jogged for the parking lot. The small plane absorbed a fresh load of travelers and vanished over the spruce spires on shuddering wings.

I walked to the shoulder of the country boulevard that ran past the airfield and waited for my brother. Ten minutes went by, then fifteen, then twenty. As the time passed, I was gored repeatedly by a species of terrible, cold-weather mosquito I had never come across before. In the time it took to beat one of their number to death, a half dozen more would perch on my arm, their engorged, translucent bellies glowing like pomegranate seeds in the cool white sun.

I'd been smacking mosquitoes for three-quarters of an hour when a red Nissan pickup truck with darkly tinted windowglass rounded the curve. It pulled to a stop in the far lane, the calved asphalt on the shoulder crunching under its tires. Matthew stepped out and crossed the road. His appearance startled me. In the year since I had last seen him, he had put on a lot of spare flesh—a set of jowls that seemed to start at his temple and a belly that could have held late-term twins. His extra weight, and the milky pallor of it, conveyed an impression of regal corpsehood, like the sculpture on the lid of an emperor's sarcophagus. I felt a mild rush of worry.

"You're late," said Matthew.

"I've been standing here for forty-five minutes."

He snorted, as though forty-five were an insufficient number of minutes for me to have been kept waiting.

"We showed up here two hours ago. Now the whole day's shot to shit."

"Look, Matthew—"

He broke in.

"My point, Alan, is that I don't just sit around out here with my hand up my ass. I had plenty on my plate today, but instead we had to come in to town and wait around, and now Bob's drunk and I'm half in the bag, and now we won't get anything done at all."

"That's good," I said. "Because I asked them specifically to hold the plane just to piss you off. I'm glad it all worked out."

"You could have called me with the status, is what I'm saying." He took his cell phone from his pocket. "Telephone, you know? They're great. You use them to tell things to people who aren't where you're at."

I wanted very much to smash my brother's nose. I picked up my bag instead. "Screw it, you asshole," I said. "I'll leave. I'll take the next plane out."

I'd walked three steps when Matthew grabbed me by the back of the neck and spun me around. His anger had evaporated, and he was giggling at me now. Nothing delights my brother like the sight of me in a rage. He kissed my eye with a rasping pressure of stubbled lip. "Who's an angry little man?" he cooed at me. "Who's an angry little man with fire in his belly?"

"I am, and you're a big fat cock," I said. "I didn't ride a plane all night to take this crap from you."

"He's all upset," said Matthew. "He's a frustrated little man."

He grabbed my duffel from me and, still laughing, marched toward the idling truck.

Through the pickup's open door, I saw the form of a man in the passenger's seat. He was slight and so deeply tanned that he was hard to make out in the dim interior.

"Alan, Bob—Bob, Alan, my baby brother," he said, though I stand six foot three, beneath a head of thinning hair, with violet half-moons of adult fatigue under my eyes.

Bob nodded once. "Good to know you, baby brother," he said. His voice creaked like an over-rosined bow. "And as the French have it, *bienvenue.*"

"Bob's a very slick ticket," said Matthew, tossing my bag into the bed with a thud. "He's a man of the world."

"Slick as a brick, and a genius in the bargain," said Bob. "I'm often told I should be president."

Matthew levered the driver's chair forward so that I could crawl into the cab's tiny rear compartment. Three large-bore rifles lay across the gun rack: the old Weatherby .300 magnum Matthew had claimed without asking from our father's estate, a sleek, black fiberglass rifle with a Nikon sight, and a cheap-looking 30.06. I had to crane my neck forward to keep my hair from touching the oiled barrels. The truck rolled onto the road.

Bob leaned around the seat to talk to me. He was older, in his sixties, I supposed.

His rucked brown cheeks were roughened with whiskers the color of old ivory, and sparse white curls poked out from under his baseball cap. "I *should* be president," Bob continued. "Don't you think? Tell me, baby brother, would you or would you not give this face your vote?" He showed me a set of teeth that looked artificially improved.

"I'd have to know where you stand on the issues," I said.

Matthew cut me a look in the rearview mirror. "I'd appreciate it if you wouldn't get him started, really."

"Alan has every right to be apprised as to where I stand," said Bob. He tapped a philosophical finger against his pursed lips and pretended to ponder his platform. After a moment, he said, "Well, here's something: I believe that anybody who wants to ought to be able to drink a cocktail with the commander-in-chief and ask the man what's what. Once a week, we hold a lottery and an ordinary citizen gets to sit down for drinks with the president. The citizen brings the booze. The constitution doesn't provide for people going around getting soused on the taxpayers' dime."

"Fair enough."

"Number two: Every municipality in the United States has a cookout the last Sunday of the month. The grills are set up on the public square. You bring the fixings, the government brings the charcoal. Why not? It's good for the community."

"Sounds sensible," I said.

"And I'm proud of number three. The federal government imposes a single sensible standard for menus in Chinese restaurants. It's my position that if you walk into the goddamned Noodle Express in Toledo, Ohio and order a number forty-two, you know that's going to be the Kung Pao Chicken, rain or shine. Any chef who won't play ball gets a kick in the rump."

"It sounds like a hell of a country," I said.

"You're damn right it does," Bob said, his voice rising. "And I've got a cabinet all picked out. You know that girl from the tire commercials? Well—"

"I'm sorry, I'm sorry," said Matthew. "But is there any way you could please shut up with this? I apologize, Bob, but how many times have I heard this bit? Just change up the fucking jukebox, please."

Bob gazed back at Matthew in wordless malice. I gathered that in the three weeks since he'd called me, the "two-man nation" he and Bob had started building here was already showing signs of ugly schism.

Matthew steered the truck through a rural abridgement of a town—a filling station, a red gambrel-roofed barn with a faltering neon sign identifying it as a pizza restaurant, and a grocery store with newspaper coupon circulars taped to the window glass. At last, Matthew spoke, trying to dispel the sour silence that had congealed in the cab.

"Hey, Alan, you didn't say anything about my new truck."

I told him I liked it.

"Just bought it. Best vehicle I've ever owned. V-6. Sport package. Got a carriage-welded, class-four trailer hitch. I'd say you're looking at a three-ton towing capacity. Maybe three and a half."

"You're really not going back to Myrtle Beach?" I asked.

"Why would I? Stick a fork in me, as far as that town's concerned. I dissolved the partnership. Hugh Auchincloss—"

"The notorious Mister Auchincloss," said Bob wearily. Matthew narrowed his eyes at him, as though he was going to say something, but didn't.

"Yes, Hugh Auchincloss, the conniver. Because of him, I took a hard fucking on this EIFS deal."

"On what deal?" I said.

"EIFS," said Matthew. "Exterior Insulation Finish System. Nonbreathable synthetic cladding. Fake stucco, is what it is, and the deal is, it fosters mold." Matthew held forth at cruel length on the perils of EIFS and moisture intrusion and the tort liabilities involved in selling condominiums that were rotten with noxious spores. Hugh Auchincloss had evidently overseen the sale and construction of five infected buildings. He had homeowners coming at him, claiming respiratory ailments, and a couple talking about brain damage to their infant kids. The courts had handed down no penalties yet, but Matthew was sure there wouldn't be much left of him when the attorneys' knives stopped flashing.

"And Kimberly, the engagement?"

"Who, Kim Jong Il?" he said in a low growl. "She's done. Dead to me."

"Why?"

"She's a gold-plated bitch is why, with an ass like a beanbag."

"You left her?"

"Something like that."

In my opinion, this was not sad news. I'd met Kimberly once, over dinner at a high-class restaurant a year ago in January. I remember that she said that she wished Matthew "would quit being such a Jew" when he declined to order a $90 bottle of champagne. Then she told us about her brother, a Marine pulling his third tour in Iraq. She said she endorsed his idea for bringing the insurgency under control, which, if I was hearing her right, involved providing drinking water only to those districts that could behave themselves, and permitting the rest of the country to parch to death or die of dysentery. Kimberly was a churchgoer, and I asked her how the water tactic would square with "Thou Shalt Not Kill." She told me that "Thou Shalt Not Kill" was from the Old Testament, so it didn't really count.

"I'm sorry," I said. "I really saw that one working out."

Matthew took a tube of sunflower seeds from the ashtray and shook a long gray dose into his mouth. Then he spit the chewed hulls into a paper cup he kept in a holder on the dash.

"To be honest with you," he said after a time, "I just don't see the rationale for anyone purchasing a vehicle that doesn't come with a carriage-welded, class-four trailer hitch."

Bob lit a cigarette and rolled the window down. I heard the sharp lisp of beer cans being opened. Bob handed one to Matthew and one to me. Then he turned around in his seat and asked me, "Baby brother, would you like to see a magic trick?"

"Sure," I said.

He picked up an orange from the floor of the truck and held it out to me.

"Feast your eyes on it, touch it. Get the image firmly in your mind. Got it?"

It was a navel orange, flattened slightly on one side.

"Now watch closely," he said, and threw the orange out the window of the truck. "Presto," he said.

"You just tossed my fucking orange, Bob," said Matthew. "I was looking forward to eating that."

"And so you can," said Bob. "Whenever you want it, it'll be waiting for you right back there."

Matthew steered the truck through a narrowing vasculature of country roads that wound into high-altitude boondocks, past trailer homes and cedar-shake cottages with reliquaries of derelict appliances and discarded automotive organs in their yards. He turned at last down a rilled trail of blond gravel. High weeds grew on the spine between the tire tracks and brushed the truck's exhaust system with a sound of light sleet.

Bob watched the forest going by. "Once we get Alan's gear stowed, we should head to the lake and get some shots in."

"Not me," said Matthew. "We already shitcanned four days this week, and nothing. I've got a house to finish up. You want to go out, go."

"You know," said Bob, "if you weren't such a know-it-all son of a bitch, you might pay some heed to the fact that it's pretty much last-chance-thirty out here as far as getting something in the freezer this year. I don't think we've got seven good days left in the season. I like to eat meat in the wintertime. Stovewood is hard on my teeth."

Matthew shrugged, but Bob had warmed to his topic, and poured forth a suite of recollections of the bitter winters he'd endured out here and the miseries of waiting for the thaw without a freezer brimming with game. Ten miles of dirt track lay between Bob's house and the blacktop road. From Matthew's cabin, it was closer to eleven, and twenty more into town. When the snow was up to the eaves of your house, you couldn't ride into town for groceries any time you felt like it. It was all right by Bob if Matthew wanted to spend his winter making the frozen trek for supermarket pork chops that tasted like silly putty while Bob fattened up on homemade venison sausage and kidney pies.

"You've lived out here awhile?" I asked Bob before the two men's bickering could start up again.

"I spent my childhood running these woods," he said. "My family owned all of this."

"When was that?"

"Well, until your fatter half persuaded it away from me."

"You want it back? Make me an offer," Matthew said. "I'll let you have it cheap."

Matthew braked the truck at Bob's house, a khaki modular home at a fork in the track. Bob made no move to get out. "Go on," said Matthew. "Don't let us keep you from making your big kill."

Bob squinted at the sky, which was opaque and the color of spackle. "Rain coming."

"Come on now, Bob, don't let a little moisture hold you back," said Matthew.

Bob did not get out. Matthew winked at me in the rearview. "Bob can't actually shoot, is the problem. His eyes are bad. He couldn't shoot his way out from under a wet napkin."

"I'm going to have them tuned up soon," said Bob. "As soon I get used to the idea of somebody chopping up my eyeballs I'll have them good as new."

"Are you staying or going?"

"What's for dinner at your place?"

"You know what: beef stroganoff."

"Hm. Stroge again. I'd hate to miss that. We'll hunt tomorrow. Drive on, sir."

The truck bumped along the path and up Matthew's "mountain," which turned out to be a low-lying hill not much loftier than a medium-volume landfill. Matthew's cabin stood in a granite clearing at the summit. Beyond it, sunlight flamed the dark surface of a pond. The cabin, to my surprise, was a modest, handsome structure built of newly peeled logs and roof shingles the color of fresh pine needles. One curious thing was that the gable ends and eaves were trimmed out with a fussy surfeit of gingerbread curlicues, ornate scrollworks, and filigreed bargeboard, giving the place the look of a tissue-paper snowflake.

"This is amazing," I said. "You built this, Matthew?"

"It was mostly Bob," Matthew said, as though it were an accusation. "Bob called the shots."

"It's a hell of a good-looking place."

Bob's features lifted in an elfin smile. "The secret ingredient is wood," he said.

Matthew led me up the front stairs, along a gangplank nailed over the bare joists of the porch. In contrast to the cabin's outward fripperies, its interior was close to raw. The floors were bare, dusty plywood and half the walls were unfinished, just pink insulation trapped behind cloudy plastic sheeting.

"Just to spite me, Bob won't hang sheetrock," said Matthew. "All day long, I'm in here, mudding joints, and he's out there with his jigsaw turning my house into a giant doily. I get after him about it, but he threatens to quit and not come back."

Matthew let out a mirthless chuckle, and with the instep of his boot he herded a pile of sawdust against the wall. "It's pathetic, isn't it? I don't guess this is where you saw me winding up."

"I'm being honest, man," I said. "I think you've got a great spot. Once you get the finishing touches on it, you'll have a little palace out here."

His vast head tilted in a leery attitude, as though he couldn't be sure I wasn't making fun of him, so I went on. "I'd kill for something like this," I said. "Look at me. I live in a studio apartment above a candle shop."

Matthew's wariness relaxed into a kind of smirking disgust. "You're still renting?"

"Yes."

"Jesus Christ. You're how old, thirty-seven?"

"I turned thirty-eight in August."

"You got a girlfriend?"

"No."

"No shit? Still nobody since what'shername? Nothing on the side?"

"No."

Matthew raised his eyebrows, gazed at the floor, loosed a long sigh. "Well, fuck," he said. "I guess things could be worse."

I spent the afternoon with Bob, finishing up the porch, while Matthew worked indoors, where he kept up a steady racket, dropping tools and swearing importantly. The boards Matthew had bought for his porch were so drastically buckled that to make them lie straight you had to strain against them until you were purple in the face. While I was grunting over a plank that was warped to a grin, Bob raised his hammer and said, heraldically, "I proclaim this to be the sorriest excuse for a piece of one-by-six decking ever touched by human hands, and I proclaim Matthew Lattimore the cheapest, laziest son of a bitch to ever tread the grand soil of Maine."

I laughed, and then I brought up something that had been on my mind. "Hey, Bob, what'd Matthew pay you for this place, if you don't mind the question."

"I do not. He paid me one hundred and eighty-nine thousand dollars in green cash."

"Ah," I said.

"How's that?"

"Nothing," I said. "I'm not surprised. You can always trust my brother to leave you holding the brown end of the stick."

"Oh, I've got no complaints," Bob said, and then drove another nail home. "The land's close to worthless, as a matter of fact. The county put its pecker to largeholders like myself. They require fifty-acre plots to build out here. You can't subdivide it. Can't develop it, can't anything with it, and it's already been timbered to hell. I got a fair price. In exchange, I've got retirement, sir! I've got new teeth in my head and a satellite dish. No, if Matthew hadn't come along when he did, I'd be at the bottom of the proverbial well of shit."

Matthew stepped onto the porch with a flask in his hand.

"So, Alan," Bob said. "You're from California. What part did you say?"

I told him that it was the northern part.

"Ah, the north! Now that's real fine. What do you do up there? I suppose you run around with men."

"I do what?"

"That you're a homosexual, sir—a queer, a punk, one of the modern Greeks."

I wasn't sure how to take this. I assured him I was not.

He nodded, and slapped another board into place. He took a nail from a pouch on his belt and sunk it in a single pistonlike stroke. "Oh no? I used to be one myself, or half of one, at least. In my twenties, I lived with my ex-wife in Annapolis, Maryland. We had a good friend in the naval academy, a corporal with a head of blond hair and a prick like a service baton. We used to take him home and wrestle him, if the mood struck us of a Saturday night."

Matthew leaned against the doorjamb and drank deeply from the flask. "He's not joking, by the way," said Matthew. "He really used to do that sort of thing."

"Oh, I did, by God, I did," said Bob. "Yes, I have fucked and sucked all across this noble land, from the burning Mojave sands to the clement shores of Lake Champlain. I took a turn with all who would have me—man, woman, and child; bird, leaf, and beast."

"God have mercy," said Matthew.

I was enjoying Bob, so I urged him on. "And what now, Bob? Have you a steady mate out here?"

He set the hammer down. "I do not, Alan. I don't have the need for one. That's why I returned to my ancestral land like a doomed old salmon-fish. I've learned in my old years that I don't really care for people. I don't like *Homo sapiens,* and I don't like to have coitus with them. Church is for noodleheads, but I'll agree with the Holy Rollers that intercourse is deplorable—somebody climbing all over you, trying to get themselves a gumdrop. Repulsive. The last time someone tricked me into it, I was angry for a week. No, sir, I'm off it for good. Of course, unless Matthew makes me a tempting offer some chill midwinter night."

"Oh, would you please shut up," Matthew said. His cheeks stood out in little quaking hillocks. For an instant I thought he would break into tears. "Oh god, my life is on fire."

We had our dinner on the porch, where a soft, warm wind was blowing in. We ate beef stroganoff that Matthew made from a kit, and drank cold gin from coffee cups because Bob felt that eating "stroge" without gin to go with it was like a kiss without a squeeze.

"Alan," Matthew said.

"Yes," I said. "What is it?"

"That money, your money from Gram Gram. Have you got it still, or did you blow it already?"

I told him that I hadn't done a thing with it at all. It was sitting in the bank.

This news invigorated him. "What is it, twenty thousand or so?"

"Yes." It was closer to forty, but I saw no need to mention that.

"Outstanding, because there's something I've been meaning to bring to your attention."

"What sort of something?"

A slow wind rattled the leaves still clinging to their limbs. On the crest of the hill, a flock of bats tumbled in the day's last light.

"This is the thing," he said. "Now listen to me. How many guys like us, like me, do you think there are out there? Ballpark figure."

"What does 'like us' mean?"

"I'm talking about jackasses who marriage isn't working out for them, they've got jobs that make them want to put a bullet in their face. Guys out in wherever, Charlotte or Brookline or Chattanooga, sitting there watching their lawns get tall. Just broke-down, broke-dick dudes with nothing to look forward to. How many guys like that you think there are?"

"It'd be tough to put a number on it, Matthew."

"Bet you there's twenty million of them, maybe more. What do these guys want? Bunch of half-dead Dagwoods. They don't want much. What they want is to do like me, come out somewhere like this, get away from all the bullshit, is all they're after."

He went on to spin a vision in which this very mountain would be gridded into a hatchwork of tiny lots, and on each lot would stand a tiny cabin, and in each cabin a lonely man would live. He was going to start a website, place ads in the back pages of men's magazines. As early as next spring, these desolated men would flock here by the hundreds to dwell in convalescent solitude, with Matthew as their uncrowned king. It would be a free and joyous land, a place where the thrill of living, unknown since childhood, would be restored to one and all. He would set up a shooting range and snowmobile trails. He might even open a mountaintop saloon where he'd show movies in the summer, and where touring bands would play.

"I'm serious," he said. "It's happening. I've already got some people on the line. I ran it past Ray Broughton, and he was wild about it. Broughton, and Tim Hayes, and Ed Little. All of them are crazy about it. They're all in for fifty."

"Fifty what?" I said.

He gave me a look. "They already sent the checks. But my point is I could let you in, even just with that twenty. If you could kick that twenty in, I'd set you up with an even share."

"I can't do it."

"Sure you can. You're not losing any money here, Alan. I'll cover it myself."

"Look, Matthew. I don't have investments, don't have a 401(k). If my practice tanks, that twenty thousand is the only thing between me and food stamps."

Matthew held up his hand, his fingers splayed and rigid. "Would you shut up a second and let me talk? Thank you. The thing you're not understanding here, Alan, is that I *make* money. I take land, and a little bit of money, and then I turn it into lots of money. That's what I do, and I am very, very good at what I do. I am not going to lose your money, Alan. What I am probably going to do is make you very rich. Now, if it wasn't for that fucking monkey Auchincloss, I wouldn't be coming to you like this, but here we are. All I'm asking is to basically just *hold* your twenty grand for a couple of months, and in return you'll be in on something that could literally change your life."

"I can't do it," I said.

He took a breath, his nostrils flaring. "Well, goddamit, Alan, what can you do? Could you go ten? Ten for a full share? Could you put in ten?"

"I'm sorry—"

"Five? Three? Two thousand? How about eight hundred, or two hundred? Would two hundred work for you, or would that break the bank?"

"Two hundred would be fine," I told him. "Put me down for that."

"Let's don't borrow trouble," said Bob. "No point in fighting over something that could never happen in a million years."

"Oh, it'll happen," said Matthew. "And I'd appreciate it if you kept out of something you don't know anything about."

"First off, there's a fifty-acre—"

Matthew swatted the idea out of the air. "Irrelevant. You file a variance, is all you do. Pay a few bucks, go to a hearing. You're done. The county's starved for development. Tax base is on the respirator. It'd sail through like corn through a goose. I'm quoting the guy at the county on that."

Bob mulled over this. "It still wouldn't work."

"Don't get down on it, Bob," said Matthew. "There'd be something in it for you, too. Who do you think would build the cabins? You'd have more money than you'd know what to do with."

Bob shook his head. "It still wouldn't work," he said.

"You've got no expertise here, Bob," Matthew said. "It's *already* working. The wheels are rolling. The ball is in play."

Bob was quiet for a moment.

"Well, for one thing," he said, "I think you'd be looking at a serious fire hazard, having all those people up here."

Matthew coughed in scorn. "What, lightning? Chimney fires? Bullshit."

"Yep, there's that," said Bob. "But what I've got in mind, if you tried to bring a couple hundred swinging dicks in here, I think what I'd probably have to do is go around with a gas can and light everybody's house on fire."

"Don't be an idiot," Matthew said.

The sound of Bob's laughing echoed in his coffee mug. "You don't know anything about me, Matthew. You don't know what I'd do."

"Here's what *I'd* do," said Matthew. "I'd crack your head open, and then I'd have you put in jail and by the time you get out you'll be wearing diapers, if that sounds like your idea of a good plan."

Bob drained his gin. Then he licked his plate a couple of times, set it down, and fixed Matthew with a smile. "Do you know who J. T. Dunlap is?"

"The guy at the service station? The guy with the bubble in his eye?"

Bob's perfect smile didn't fade. "That's right. Go ask J. T. Dunlap what went on between his brother and Bob Brown. He'll tell you some things you ought to know before you go around making threats."

For all the joy that Matthew finds in provoking other people, he has never been a violent man. My brother is comfortable only in contests he is sure to win, and the chaos of physical violence muddies his calculi of acceptable risk. In his school years, I had seen Matthew run from boys whose throats he could have danced on rather than take his chances in a fight.

Matthew chewed his bottom lip and stared at Bob with cautious, hooded eyes. Then he stood up and hurled his plate against the side of the cabin. It bloomed into smithereens just below the porch light. He stood there long enough to watch a pale clod of creamed noodles fall wetly to the floor. Then he walked inside, slamming the door hard enough to make the gutters chime.

Bob clicked his tongue and said it was time to turn her in. He stood and held his hand out to me. I took it with some reluctance. "So we'll see you dark and early, then," said Bob. "And if Mister Grouchy Bear isn't in a mood to hunt, then you and me will just have to go ourselves. *Bonsoir.*" Bob straightened his cap and winked at me and strolled into the night.

Matthew's only furniture was the sheetless mattress he was sprawled on in the center of the living-room floor. He did not stir when I came in. I folded myself into the warm embayment formed of my brother's knees and outflung arms and fell into a sturdy sleep.

The door creaked open before dawn. "Out of the fartsack, gentlemen," said Bob, clapping his hands. "Come on, get to it, boys."

Bob tramped to the stove. He lit a lantern and boiled water for coffee. I rose and dressed. The air in the cabin was dense with cold.

Matthew hadn't moved. I rocked his shoulder with my foot.

"Leave me alone," said Matthew.

"All righty," Bob said brightly. "The big man's sleeping in. Alan?"

I nudged him again. Matthew sighed a quick, harsh sigh and got up with a crashing of bedclothes and thudding of knees and feet. He pulled on a camouflage bib, a parka, and an elaborate hunter's vest, busy with zippered compartments, ruffled across the breast with cartridge loops. Matthew retrieved the guns from the pickup and carried them to Bob's old white Ford, which sat in the driveway, an aluminum skiff on the trailer it was towing. We climbed in and rode off down the hill. I sat wedged between Bob and my brother. Matthew rested his head against the dew-streaked window, drowsing, or pretending to. Bob was ebullient. Last night's hostilities seemed to have passed from his mind. He prattled at a manic clip on topics ranging from rumors of prehistoric, sixty-foot sharks living along the Mariana Trench to the claim of a Hare Krishna he had met that poor black Americans were white slave owners in their prior lives.

We rode for half an hour on a two-lane state highway, and then Bob turned the Ford down a narrow road, where the leprous trunks of silver birch flared in the headlights. The road carried us to the shore of a lake. Bob nimbly backed the trailer to the water's edge and winched the boat down a mossy slip into the water. Bob and I carried the gear into the boat. Matthew took a seat near the bow with the guns across his lap, facing east, where the sky was rusting up with the approaching dawn.

Bob pulled the cord on the motor, and the skiff skimmed out of the cove. We headed north, hugging the shore, past worlds of marsh grass, and humped expanses of pink granite that looked like corned beef hash. After a twenty-minute ride, Bob stopped the boat at a stretch of muddy beach where he said he'd had some luck before. We pulled the skiff ashore, and Matthew and I followed Bob into the tree line.

Bob browsed the woods on quiet, nimble feet, stopping now and again to check for sign. At the edge of a grassy clearing, Bob waved us over to have a look at a pine sapling whose limbs had been stripped by a rutting buck. He knelt, and scooped a handful of deer shits into his palm. He raised his hand to his face with such savor and relish that for a moment I thought that he was going to tip the turds into his mouth. "That's fresh all right," he said, and cast them away. "I think we'll make some money here."

We sat in ambush back in the trees, in view of the wrecked sapling, and waited. A loon moaned on the lake. Crows bitched and cackled overhead. Before the dawn had fully broken, a fine, cold rain started sifting down. We drew our collars in. The rainwater slid from our chins down the front of our shirts. Nothing moved in the clearing. After two hours, a sparrow walked out of a bush and then walked back in again.

Far be it from me to guess at what goes on in my brother's rash head, but it seemed to me that the black and hollow silence enclosing him that morning was something new for him. In Matthew's idle moments, I could usually see on his face the turnings of distant gears—negotiations being schemed over, old lovers being recalled, iced tumblers of strong alcohol being thirstily imagined. I had never seen his face this way before, slack and unblinking, a vacant, lunar emblem of irreparable regret.

"Doing okay?" I asked him.

"Yeah, of course," he said in a listless monotone. "No sweat."

It took Bob until ten o'clock to decide that nothing was happening for us there. We trudged back to the skiff, and Bob drove us to the far end of the lake, where he knew about a big deer stand which would at least get our asses off of the wet ground. Instead, we killed another couple of hours huddled together up there in the stand, spying down on some empty woods while the sky kept leaking on us. I didn't talk and neither did Matthew. At one point Bob said, "This is why they call it hunting," and an hour or so later he said it again.

Around noon, Bob broke out the lunch he'd brought along, which was bologna sandwiches with cold wads of margarine lumped under the soggy bread. Out of swooning hunger and politeness, I ate my sandwich. Matthew took one bite of his and pitched it off the stand. Bob saw him do it but didn't say anything.

We got back in the boat and thrummed out over the lake, which was stuccoed just faintly with light rain. We skimmed across the broads to a wide delta where a river paid out into a marshy plain, a spot where Bob claimed to have killed a buck four or six or eight years ago. The bank sloped up to a little rocky promontory. We hiked up there and got down behind some big white pines. We hadn't been there long when Matthew sat up, rapt. "There we go," he said.

On the far side of the delta, a large bull moose had stepped from the tree line and was drinking in the shallows, maybe three hundred yards away, an impossible distance. "Jesus, shit," Bob said in a whisper, and then he made an urgent motion for one of us to slip back down the bank and get the moose into clear range. But Matthew seemed not to hear. He got on his feet, raised his rifle, took a breath, and fired. The moose's forelegs crumpled beneath it, and an instant later I saw the animal's head jerk as the sound of the shot reached him. The moose tried to struggle upright but fell again. The effect was of a very old person trying to pitch a heavy tent. It tried to stand, and fell, and tried, and fell, and then gave up its strivings.

Matthew rubbed his eye with the heel of his hand. He gave us a quizzical look, as though he half suspected that the whole thing was a trick that Bob and I had somehow rigged up. It surprised me that he didn't promptly launch into the gloating fanfare and brash self-tribute that generally attend the tiniest of his successes. "Trippy," was all he said as he gazed toward his kill.

"One shot—are you shitting me?" said Bob. "That's the goddamnedest piece of marksmanship I've ever seen."

We made our way down to the carcass. The moose had collapsed in a foot of icy river water and had to be dragged onto firm ground before it could be dressed. What a specimen it was, shaggy brown velvet going on forever, twelve hundred pounds at least, Bob guessed. Matthew and I waded out to where the creature lay. We passed a rope under his chest. We looped the other end around a tree on the bank, using it as a makeshift pulley, and then tied the rope to the stern of the skiff. Bob gunned the outboard, and Matthew and I stood calf-deep in the shallows heaving on the line. By the time we'd gotten the moose to shore, our palms were puckered and torn raw, and our boots were full of water.

Matthew took Bob's hunting knife and bled the moose from the throat, and then made a slit from the bottom of the rib cage to the jaw, revealing the gullet and a pale, corrugated column of windpipe. The scent was powerful. It brought to mind the dark, briny smell that seemed always to hang around my mother when I was a child. Gorge rose faintly in my throat.

Matthew's face was intent, nearly mournful, as he worked, and he didn't say a word. Gingerly, he opened the moose's belly, careful not to puncture the intestines or the stomach. With Bob's help, he carefully dragged out the organs, and Bob set aside the liver, the kidneys, and the pancreas. The hide proved devilishly hard to remove. To get it loose, Bob and I had to brace against the creature's spine and pull with all our might while Matthew sawed at the connective tissues. Then Matthew sawed the hams and shoulders free. We had to lift the legs like pallbearers to get them to the boat. Blood ran from the meat and down my shirt with horrible warmth.

When we had the moose loaded in the boat, the hull rode low in the water. So the bow wouldn't swamp on the ride back to the truck, Matthew, the most substantial ballast of the three of us, sat in the stern and ran the kicker. Clearing the shallows, he opened up the throttle, and we sped off with a big white whale's fluke of churned water arcing out behind us. The wind blew his clotted hair from his forehead. The old unarmored smile I knew from Matthew's early childhood brightened his face. His lips parted in the familiar compact bow. He raised his eyebrows and wagged his tongue at me in pleasure. There is no point in my trying to describe the love I can still feel for my brother when he looks at me this way, when he is briefly free from worries over money, or his own significance, or how much liquor is left in the bottle in the freezer. Ours is not the kind of brotherhood I would wish on other men, but we are blessed with a single, simple gift. Though sometimes I think I know less about Matthew than I do about a stranger passing on the street, when I am with him in his rare moments of happiness, I can feel his pleasure, his sense of fulfillment, as though I were in his very heart. The killing had restored him, however briefly, to the dream of how he'd imagined life would be for him here. As the skiff glided over the dimming lake, I could feel how satisfying the gridded rubber handle of the Evinrude must have felt humming in his hand, and the air rushing through his whiskered cheeks, drying the moose's fluids and the brine of his own exertions. I could sense the joy of his achievement in having felled the animal, all the more pure because he had not made much of it, and his pride in knowing that its flesh would nourish two men until the spring.

With the truck loaded, and the skiff rinsed clean, we rode back to Matthew's hill. It was past dinnertime when we reached the cabin. Our stomachs yowled. Matthew asked if Bob and I wouldn't mind trimming and wrapping up his share of the meat while he put some steaks on the grill. Bob said sure, but that before he did any more work he was going to need to sit in a dry chair for a little while and drink two beers. While Bob was doing that, Matthew waded into the bed of the Ford, which was heaped nearly flush with the maroon dismantlings. With the knife in his hand, he browsed the mass. Then he bent over, sawed at the carcass for a while, and then held up a tapered log of flesh that looked like a peeled boa constrictor. "Tenderloin. You ever seen anything so pretty, Alan? If you had a thousand dollars, you couldn't buy yourself one of these, not fresh anyway."

He carried the loin to the porch and lit the grill. With a sheet of plywood and a pair of sawhorses, Bob and I rigged up a butcher station on the driveway in the headlights of Bob's truck.

I'd had enough of work by then. A swooning fatigue was settling on me. Not long into the job, I was not sure I'd feel it if I ran the knife into my hand. Bob, too, was unsteady on his feet. When he blinked, his eyes stayed closed a while. We had been at it for a time, when I began to take conscious notice of the dark aroma that had been gathering by degrees in the air around us, a sour diarrheal scent. The awful thought struck me that the old man, in his exhaustion, had let his bowels give way. I said nothing. A while later, Bob wrinkled his nose and looked at me. "Are you farting over there?" he said.

I told him no.

"What *is* that? My God, it smells like someone cracked open a sewer." He sniffed at his sleeve, then at his knife, then at the block of meat in front of him. "*Hruk,*" he said, recoiling. "Oh, good Christ—it's off."

He went around to the truck bed and stood on the tailgate, taking up pieces at random at putting them to his face. "Son of a bitch. It's contaminated. It's something deep in the meat."

I sniffed my fingers, and caught a whiff of grave breath, the unmistakable stink of decay.

Out on the porch, Matthew had a radio turned up loud, and had set out a bottle of wine to breathe. On the patio table, three filets the size of wall clocks rested on paper plates, already pink and sodden. Matthew was ladling out servings of yellow rice when we walked up.

"Not possible," he said calmly, after Bob broke the news. "We broke it down perfectly. I'm sure of it. Nothing spilled at all. You saw."

"It was sick," said Bob. "That thing was dying on its feet when you brought it down."

"Oh, bull-*shit*. You figured that out, how?"

"Contaminated, I promise you," said Bob. "I should have known it when the skin hung on there like it did. He was bloating up with something, just barely holding on. The second he died, and turned that infection loose, it just started going wild."

Matthew rubbed his thumb across the slab of meat he'd intended for himself, and licked at the juice. "Tastes okay to me," he said. With a brusque swipe of his knife, he cut off a dripping pink ingot. He speared it with his fork and touched it to his tongue. "Totally fine. A little gamy, maybe, but they don't call it game for no reason. What?"

He licked it once more and then he squinted at the meat, the way a jeweler might look at a gem he could not quite identify.

"Poison," said Bob.

"No big thing, we go back out tomorrow," I said. "You'll get another one, no sweat."

But Matthew was not listening. He cocked his head and held it still, as though the sound of something in the woods beyond the cabin had suddenly caught his ear. Then he turned back to the table and slipped the fork into his mouth.

Roddy Doyle

BLACK HOODIE

MY GIRLFRIEND IS NIGERIAN, kind of, and when we go through the shops, we're followed all the way. We stop—the security guards stop. We go up the escalator—they're three steps behind us, and there's another one waiting at the top. We look at something, say, a shoe, and they all look at us looking at the shoe. And people—ordinary people, like—they see the security guards looking at us, and they stop and start looking at us, in case something good's going to happen. You're never lonely if you're with a black girl, or even if your hoodie is black. There's always someone following you—"Move along, move along"—making sure you're getting your daily exercise.

I'm not complaining. I'm just stating the facts.

That's the first thing the Guards—the real cops, not the security guards—it's the first thing they learn when they're doing their training down the country. How to say "Move along" in 168 different languages. Even before they learn how to eat their jumbo rolls without getting butter all over their shirts.

I said she was Nigerian, kind of. I didn't mean she was kind of Nigerian. I meant she's kind of my girlfriend. She's lovely and, I have to admit, I kind of like the attention. No one really noticed me until I started going with her, kind of.

Now they all look, and you can see it in their faces; they're thinking, "There's a white fella with a black girl," or something along those lines. I'm the white fella. It's better than nothing.

I'm dead into her. I'd love it if she were my girlfriend—full-time, like. My da says I should just go ahead and ask her. But I don't know. That's what he must have done, a hundred years ago, and he ended up with my ma. So, I'm not sure. What if she says no?

But it's a bit gay at the moment. We're *friends*—do you know what I mean? And that's grand; it's not too bad. But I'd love to, like, hold her a bit and kiss her.

I'm not telling you her name. And that means I can't use my own name either. Because, how many Nigerian girls is the average Irish teenager going to be hanging around with, even here in multicultural, we-love-the-fuckin'-foreigners Dublin? If I give my name, I might as well give hers. So, no.

So, there we are, myself and my Nigerian friend, and we're walking through the shop, being tailed by the Feds. And meanwhile, our friend, who's in a—

And now, there's another problem. There's a fella in a wheelchair in the story. How many male teenagers in the greater Dublin area share their leisure time with young men in wheelchairs and Nigerian women?

Our friend is in a wheelchair, but he doesn't need it. It's his brother's. His brother is in McDonald's, waiting for us. He doesn't have much of a choice, because we have his wheelchair. And he needs it, badly. There's a ginormous milkshake cup in front of him. It's empty. The shake's in him, and he's bursting. He's full of vanilla and the jacks is down the back, miles—sorry, kilometers away.

And his brother has his wheelchair. He's in the same shop as us—that's me and the Nigerian bird. And while the Feds follow me because (a) I'm with a black person, and (b) I'm wearing a hoodie, he's robbing everything he can stretch to, because (a) he's in the wheelchair, and (b) he's wearing glasses. And no one follows him. In fact, everyone wants to help him.

It's an experiment. Market research. I'll explain in a minute.

His brother is sliding toward the jacks when we get back to McDonald's. He's halfway there and, so far, €8.56 has been thrown at him.

Let me explain.

We aren't robbing the stuff because we want it, or just for the buzz. No. We are a mini-company. Three of us are in Transition Year, in school. The brother who actually owns the wheelchair isn't. He's in Sixth Year. We used to call him Superman, but he asked us to stop after Christopher Reeve died; it was upsetting his ma whenever she answered the landline. "Is Superman there?" So, fair enough; we stopped.

Anyway, as part of our Transition Year program, me and Ms. Nigeria and not-Superman's brother had to form a mini-company, to help us learn about the real world and commerce and that. And we didn't want to do the usual stuff, like making sock hangers and Rice Krispie cakes. So, we sat at a desk and, watched closely by our delightful teacher, Ms. They-Don't-Know-I-Was-Drunk-Last-Night, we came up with the idea, and the name.

Black Hoodie Solutions.

CHAPTER TWO

I'm not all that sure about Transition Year. Like, learning to drive is on the curriculum, and that sounds a lot better than maths or religion. But then you find out there's no car. Mr. I'm-So-Cool-In-My-Jacket says something about insurance and us being too young, and we end up learning to drive by looking at the blackboard. I'm serious. He draws a circle on the board with a piece of red chalk.

"That now, ladies and gentlemen, is—a—roundabout."

And he shows us how to *negotiate* it, with a piece of white chalk.

So, it's good and it's bad. Sound Recording is cool, and First Aid is good crack. Bed-Sit Cookery isn't too bad. But Teen Thoughts! It's so bad, so—worse than shite. The teacher, Ms. I'm-Not-Really-A-Teacher, sits on top of her desk and says something like, "Hey, guys. Girls masturbate too. Surprised?" And she expects us to discuss it. I'm not making this up. She just sits there, waiting. "Anybody?"

Then there's the mini-companies. They're a good idea, I suppose. But it would make a lot more sense if you could, say, open a shop—a real one, like—and sell CDs and DVDs, or whatever, for a week or two. Or open a restaurant, or start Dublin Bus or something. You'd definitely know more about your aptitudes and stuff after that. But, I know, it's not realistic. But what's the compromise? Rice Krispie cakes and babysitting. Like, you babysit for a bit, add up the amount of money you make, and this gives you a good idea of what's it like to be the boss of Microsoft. Yeah; maybe.

Anyway. We're having none of it. Me and Ms. Nigeria and our friend whose brother owns the wheelchair. He's allergic to chocolate, for a start. Something really disgusting happens to his skin if he even, like, looks at a Rolo. So that rules out the Rice Krispie cakes. Anyway, another group gets to that one before us, and they look so chuffed you'd swear they'd just invented eBay. And no way would I ever babysit, I don't care how much you pay me. Babies are weird.

So, like, we kind of just sit there while the other groups grab all the ace business opportunities. Painted light bulbs; shopping for old people; washing cars.

We're the last. And Ms. They-Don't-Know-I-Was-Drunk-Last-Night is staring at us, her pen, like, held right over her list, waiting for our brainwave.

And it comes.

"Stereotyping," says Ms. Nigeria.

"What?" says Ms. They-Don't-Know etc. "I mean—what do you mean?"

She puts on her big, interested face—*Interesting!* She's being extra-nice for the black girl. She looks like she might fall over.

"Well," says the young woman I secretly love, "we're constantly being labelled."

She always talks like that, like she's on the news or something. I like it—a lot.

"Oh, excellent!" says Ms. etc. "You're going to make labels. Accessorize."

"Well," says the Nigerian newsreader. "No, actually. You misunderstood."

Ms. They-Don't-Know looks up *misunderstood* in the dictionary in her head. It takes a while—it's way at the back, behind her childhood memories and last night's empties. I watch the sweat climb out of her forehead.

"We're being clever, are we—Name Omitted?" she says.

"No," says Name Omitted. "I'm quite happy to explain."

I'd be quite happy to lie down and lick her feet. But it probably isn't the time or the place.

"Go on, for God's sake," says Ms. They-Don't-Know. "Go on."

"Well," says Name Omitted.

I sit up, like I know what's happening. Name Omitted waves her hand.

"We are all labelled and stereotyped," she says. "Automatically. We don't have to say or do anything. Even you are, Miss."

"Me?"

"Yes."

"How am I—stereotyped?" she asks. The big word comes out, slowly, like a table-tennis ball out of a magician's mouth.

"Well," says Ms. Nigeria. "You look like you—"

"Don't!" says Ms. They-Don't.

She looks like she's going to cry.

"Just—go on."

"Okay," says Ms. Nigeria. "For example. I walk into a shop and the security staff immediately decide that I am there to shoplift."

"Because you're black?"

"Because I'm young," says Ms. Nigeria. "And, yes, because I'm black."

Ms. They-Don't-Know has recovered, a bit.

"What has this got to do with your mini-company?"

"Well," says Name Omitted. "Can you imagine the wastage of man-hours and goodwill—oh, all sorts of things—that results directly from this?"

She certainly knows her onions—whatever that means.

"Go on," says Ms. They-Don't-Know.

"Well," says Name Omitted, "Myself and my colleagues here"—and she points at me and the other fella—"are going to establish a consultancy firm, to advise retail outlets on stereotyping of young people, and best practice toward its elimination."

And that's how we end up in Pearse Street Police Station.

CHAPTER THREE

It's me who comes up with the name, Black Hoodie Solutions. I'm wearing a black hoodie and my Nigerian lover is black and she's got a hoodie too—kind of a girl one—and the other fella's got one too. So that's *Black Hoodie.* And the *Solutions* bit—it just sounds cool. So, there you go—Black Hoodie Solutions. Ms. They-Don't-Know writes it down, and the bell goes.

Next thing you know, we're robbing shops.

And it's cool; business is brisk. The manager of the Spar near the school is a bit freaked when we bring back the stuff we've just stolen, but she's quite impressed when she sees the CCTV footage of her security muppet walking after Ms. Nigeria's arse—true—while I'm right behind him, the hoodie off, taking four packs of microwave popcorn and an *NME.* She even pays us a tenner and Cornetto, each—the Cornettos, not the tenner.

But we're happy; we're ahead. A whole tenner, no overhead—the Irish economy doesn't know what hit it.

We stay local, at first: the Londis, the chemist's, Fat Larry's Pet Shop—not his real name but he is fat. We rob a tortoise and two rabbits out of Fat Larry's, and we bring them back. It's a bit tricky, this one, because Fat Larry is his own security man, so we're more or less accusing him of racism and sexism, and very stupid–ism. But he takes it on the chins and hands over our consultancy fee, in 20c pieces, and tells us we can keep the tortoise. He insists on it. His words still ring in my ears: "Yis can shove it up your arses."

So there you go. By the end of Week One, we're laughing, as my da always says—although I've never heard him laugh. Except that one time when my ma caught her fingers in the toaster—he laughed a bit then.

Anyway. Ms. Nigeria hands our weekly report to Ms. They-Don't-Know-I-Was-Drunk-Yet-Again-Last-Night. Three pages, a black folder, logo and all. Not-Superman in the wheelchair does the logo for us, on his computer. It's cool—hoodie shape, arms out, hood up. But how come people in wheelchairs are always brilliant on computers? What's the story there? And what were they good at before there were any computers?

Anyway. Ms. They-Don't-Know is impressed, but a bit suspicious.

She looks at me.

"So," she says. "What's next?"

"Well," says Ms. Nigeria. "We're taking it to a new level."

"Yes," I agree.

"Oh shite," says not-Superman's brother.

And that's where you meet us, back in Chapter One, robbing the bigger places in town—him in his brother's wheelchair, doing the larceny bit, while me and Ms. Nigeria drag the muppets up and down the escalators, through all the bras and plasma screens.

Shop One is a sweetshop, on Henry Street. All goes to plan. But we're so impressed with the goods that not-Superman's brother manages to smuggle out that we decide to eat them. It's strictly a once-off decision, and good for morale. Then we drop not-Superman off at McDonald's and head off for Shop Two, also on Henry Street. We take turns in the wheelchair till we reach our target. It's a large department store, much loved by Dublin's mammies; and, again, all goes to plan. We leave the premises, by different exits. We reconvene, give not-Superman back his wheelbarrow. And we re-enter, to hand back the goods and negotiate our consultancy fee.

We ask Svetlana at the information desk for the manager. And, while we wait, we smile and—yeah—we giggle. And I'm really close to grabbing Ms. Nigeria's hand and asking her to go with me, when another hand grabs my shoulder and I nearly wet myself. I think I might yelp or something—I'm not sure.

There are four hands, one for each of us.

Four big hands. They belong to three big men and a huge woman. They're all in Garda uniforms, so it's a fair bet they're Guards.

I yelp again—or something.

"Mind if we look in the bag, lads?" says one of the Feds. It might even be my one; I feel his breath on my neck.

The bag is on not-Superman's lap.

"Eh," he says. "No."

But they're already gawking into the bag—it's my schoolbag, actually; my prints are all over it. A big hand goes in, and takes out (1) a pair of shin guards; (2) a red high-heeled shoe, and (3) a Holy Communion dress.

"You took them from this shop, didn't you?" says the lady Garda.

"No," says Ms. Nigeria. "Actually, we didn't. We're still in the shop."

And we can tell; it's on their big faces—she's caught them rapid.

But they still drag us down to Pearse Street Station.

CHAPTER FOUR

Have you ever seen a guy in a wheelchair wearing handcuffs? With his hands behind his back? I mean, they could lock him to the side of the chair; he's not going anywhere. But, no, they cuff him the same way they cuff the rest of us, hands behind the back. Maybe they have to—they can't discriminate against him, or something. I don't know.

Anyway. It takes them forever to get him into the back of the van.

"I didn't do anything," he says.

"None of us *did* anything," says Ms. Nigeria.

She's right. If he's innocent, that means the rest of us have to be guilty. He's ratting on us before he's even in the van. He should keep his mouth shut and be a man—like me.

If I speak, I'll start crying. But no one else knows that. My lips are sealed. My eyes are—whatever. I look across at Ms. Nigeria. I smile. She smiles back. I'll ask her to go with me when we get to the station.

Not-Superman is in the van. There's even a special seat belt for his chair. They must arrest the wheelchair people a lot more often than I'd have expected.

We're on our way down Henry Street, at seven kph. It isn't nice. Sitting like that, like, with a seat belt, with your hands behind your back—it's kind of horrible. The cuffs are digging into me. And I want to go to the toilet. And I'm scared. Two huge words keep going on and off in my head. OH SHIT, OH SHIT, OH SHIT.

But I smile across at Ms. Nigeria.

"All right?"

"Perfectly all right."

But she's not perfectly all right. I think I know her well enough by now. She's planking too.

But you should see the state of not-Superman's brother. He's mumbling in a language that isn't English, and I don't think it's Irish. I sit beside him in French, and it's not that one either. I stop looking at him. I'm afraid his head will start spinning, like your woman in *The Exorcist*. I wish I'd never seen it. OH SHIT, OH SHIT.

I smile at Ms. Nigeria. She smiles back. She even laughs.

"Mad," I say.

"Yes," she says back. "Preposterous."

Then we get to the station. And it stops being funny. OH SHIT, OH SHIT, OH SHIT. There's one of those smells, like, and a lot of noise and a guy going mad somewhere in the back—in a *cell*. And I keep thinking that I'll be going in there with him soon, and the handcuffs really hurt, and it's getting harder not to shake.

They leave us all in a corner.

"Don't budge," says my Garda.

"No," I say, before I can stop myself.

He's a bollix.

My chair is kind of broken. I have to lean over on one side to stop it from collapsing. It must look like I'm going to be sick or something.

"They've no case," says Ms. Nigeria.

"No," I agree.

"We actually took nothing," she says.

I'm with her all the way. And I let her know it.

"Yeah."

"The sweets," says not-Superman's brother.

He's trying to wipe one of his eyes with his shoulder.

"What?"

"We took the sweets," he says.

"We ate them," says his brother.

OH SHIT, OH SHIT. I can suddenly taste them. They were all right—not really as nice as cheap sweets, if you follow me. But, anyway, they're back in my mouth—the taste, not the actual sweets. I don't want to breathe. And I'm not the only one. We're all afraid the Guards will smell the theft on our breaths.

A new one, not in a uniform, but he's definitely a Garda—there's something about the shape of his head. Anyway, he's there. And he's hard. And he points. At me.

"You. Up."

I stand.

"No," he says. "You."

He points at not-Superman's little brother.

"Me?"

"Up. Over here."

"Don't say anything," Ms. Nigeria whispers.

"You," says the new Garda.

He's pointing at Ms. Nigeria.

"Shut your sub-Saharan mouth."

"Excuse me?" she says; but it's not really a question.

He stares at her.

"You can't say that," she says.

He still stares at her—at us—at her. He opens a door behind him without looking at it.

"In."

But he stands right on front of the door. Not-Superman's brother has to squeeze past him. He follows him in.

The door shuts. I wait for the screams—I do. OH SHIT, OH SHIT.

"He can't say that," says Ms. Nigeria.

My Garda is back. I'm kind of glad to see him.

"Right, lads," he says. "Names, addresses, the parents' mobile numbers."

He stands in front of Ms. Nigeria.

"The jungle drums in your case, love."

I told you already, it stops being funny.

CHAPTER FIVE

I just want to talk. I mean, I don't. But I can't help it. The cop asks for my name and address. The brainy dude in my head, who always knows what I should say and do, but *after*—d'you know what I mean? Anyway, he's telling me to keep my mouth shut, ask for a lawyer—the stuff you see on the telly, like. But I give the cop my name and address, and my mobile, and my da's mobile, and his job, and my granny's trousers size—and everything. I can't help it. I want him to like me, and I don't—he's a racist bollix. But I'm really scared. And—did I say this already?—I can't help it.

I look at Ms. Nigeria, and I don't think I'll be asking her to go with me. Not just yet. She's angry—you should see her eyes. But she's calm. It's amazing. She's a girl— she's *the* girl, like, the only one in this part of the cop shop. But she's the only one not blabbing or crying, or both. She stares at the cop. He's not even looking her but he feels it. Like, the rays from her eyes. They burn the arse hair off him, or something.

He looks at her.

"What?"

"You have no right to speak like that," she says.

"Like what?" he says.

It's like, for a second, she's the cop. But then it changes. He catches up with her—that's what it looks like. He stands up real straight, so he's looking down at her and all of us.

"If I was you, love," he says, "I'd keep my trap shut for a while."

She looks back at him.

"And don't worry," he says. "We don't torture people in this country. Amn't I right, lads?"

I dip the head before he can look at me properly. But then I do it—I feel it, in my neck: I'm telling myself to look back at him. And I do. And—oh shite.

"Wipe it," he says.

"What?"—I have to cough a bit before the word gets out.

"The look off your face," he says. "Before someone else wipes it for you."

I look back at him for as long as I can. Then I look away.

"Good man."

I have the shakes, bad. Like, my handcuffs are rattling against the back of the chair. But—this is weird—I'm happy. Just for a bit. Ms. Nigeria isn't doing any more protesting and your man telling me to wipe the look off my face—I've kind of caught up with her. I'm feeling a bit brave.

The door opens.

OH SHIT OH SHIT.

"You."

It's me.

"You."

It's definitely me. He's pointing at me.

Not-Superman's brother just about makes it to the nearest chair. He kind of crawls up onto it, like it's a huge mouth and he wants to be eaten.

It's my turn.

OH SHIT.

I stand up—I can.

I walk. I look at the plainclothes cop as I get nearer. I don't—I do. I do and I don't. I look at his shoulder. I walk past him. Into his room.

A desk and two chairs. That's the room. Not even a WANTED poster or one of those two-way mirrors. Oh, and there's a video camera, on a tripod, beside the table.

I don't sit down.

"Sit down."

I sit down. He leans over the table. I can see his teeth.

"Another of the hoodies," he says.

He goes to the camera. He looks at the screen thing. He adjusts the lens.

"Put the hood up," he says.

"Why?"

He stares at me.

"I can't," I say. "My hands are cuffed."

He goes behind me and pulls the hood over my head. It's right down to my eyes. He takes off my handcuffs. He holds my arms behind my back—hard, like. He lets go. He goes back to the camera.

I take the hoodie off my head.

"Put it back," he says.

"Why?" I ask.

He stares.

My hands are shaking, sore. I put the hood back up.

"That's the ticket," he says. "Any tattoos?"

"Me?"

"Yeah."

"No."

"Ah well," he says. "You still look the part."

He stares at me.

He turns the camera on. He sits.

"Thursday, fourteenth of November," he says. "Name?"

I tell him.

"Age?"

I tell him.

"Would you take the hood down, please?" he says.

I don't. Like, I don't know what he really wants me to do.

"The hood," he says.

I lift my hand. I pull the hood back off my head. There's nothing else I can do. I'm only copping on why he made me put it up in the first place. It's on video, like—the proof. I'm wearing a hoodie. I must be guilty.

CHAPTER SIX

He speaks without looking at me.

"Tell me what occurred this afternoon," he says.

Now he looks.

"Take your time."

"Like…" I start.

It should be easy. I know exactly what happened. There's nothing I have to hide—except the sweets.

"Like," I start again.

But I don't know how to start. How to make it sound straightforward and normal. He thinks I'm guilty already. And so do I. That's the problem.

"We were doing a project," I say.

It's nothing to do with the sweets. It's the way it's all done. The camera, making me put up my hoodie. I must have done something. I deserve to be here.

I know I don't. I *know*—in my head, like. I'm innocent—forget about the sweets for a sec. But I feel guilty. The camera is telling me that, and the soreness where the cuffs were. The way I look—I deserve this.

You're probably thinking, "Jesus, he's giving in quickly. Thank God he wasn't in the War of Independence, or whatever. We'd never have won it." But I don't give in. I tell him nothing that didn't actually happen. But I feel all the time that he's going to catch me out.

"Project?" he says.

"Yeah."

I'm messing with the string of my hoodie, in front of the camera. I stop.

"Tell me a bit about this project," he says.

"It's a mini-company," I say.

"Buying and selling," he says.

"No," I say.

"Selling, anyway. Robbing and selling."

"No."

"No?"

"Not really," I say.

He shifts in his chair. His foot kind of slides across my shin.

"The goods were in your possession—"

He says my name.

"We were still in the shop," I say.

"You'd left."

"We came back."

"Okay," he says. "Why?"

"To give them back," I say. "That's the project, like. It's about stereotyping."

He looks like he wants to lean over and whack me. A lot of people look that way when they hear that word *stereotype.*

"Go on," he says.

"Like," I say. "Me and—Name Omitted—walked around the shop and because of the way we look—"

I hold the hoodie and shake it a bit.

"The hoodie and her skin and that, the security guards followed us all over the place. And the fella in the wheelchair took the stuff in the bag, the dress and the shoe and—I forget the other thing."

"Shin guards," he says.

"Yeah," I say. "Thanks. He took them and no one watched him because he doesn't look the type and they left him alone."

"Go on."

"That's it," I say.

I'm hoping he's heard enough. If I go much further, I'll be telling him that (a) he got it wrong, and (b) he's a racist. But—

"Go on," he says.

I have to. The camera's on me.

"Well," I say. "Like, we brought the stuff back into the shop. And then we were going to explain what we'd done and show them how we'd done it. How they were losing money because of their prejudices. And they'd pay us a fee."

He's looking at me. I don't think he's happy. But, funny, I don't care that much. I'm kind of proud of myself. I've explained what we did. I think I've been clear.

"We'd done it already," I tell him—I'm shaking a bit. "In other shops, like. And they paid us."

I wish Ms. Nigeria was with me. I think she'd be impressed. I know I am. I'm going to do Law after the Leaving.

He stands up. He turns off the camera. OH SHIT. He's going to batter me— you should see his face.

He stares—he stares. He's good at it.

"Sorry about that," I say.

"Fuckin' gobshite," he says.

He walks across to the door. It opens before he gets there. It's the lady Guard.

"The parents are here," she says.

I know it's not my ma. She'd never come out, not even to save me from the electric chair. Not even to watch.

It's my da. He smiles like it hurts. But he smiles.

"Son."

"Da."

"A bit of bother."

"Yeah. Sorry."

"We'll deal with it."

Just now, he's great. He's legend.

I look across at Ms. Nigeria. She still looks angry and lovely and—

"I have to do something, Da," I say.

He speaks very quietly. He actually whispers.

"It might be better if we just go."

"Not yet," I say. "I have to do it."

He decides—he nods.

"You know best," he says. "I'm with you."

The plainclothes Garda has his back to us. He's walking away, to the front of the station.

"Excuse me," I say. "Excuse ME."

He stops. He turns. I hear my da say it.

"Oh shit."

CHAPTER SEVEN

The Garda turns but he takes his time. It's like a film, a good one, like—it scares the crap out of me. There's complete silence. Even the buses outside have stopped—it feels like that. He doesn't look at me, or anyone. And his hands—they're kind of hanging at his hips. He's like your man, Henry Fonda, in *Once Upon a Time in the West*. He's going for his guns. Just as well he doesn't have any.

It's still frightening but. All I can hear is the squeak of one of his shoes on the floor. Or maybe the squeak comes out of me, or even my da—I'm not sure.

He stops—and he stares. At me.

"Yes?"

He says that.

"Eh."

That's me—I say that.

"What?" he says.

He doesn't look at my da, or anyone else. Just me. A man walks into the station behind him. It must be Ms. Nigeria's da. He's black, like. And there's a woman behind him. She's black too. That'll be the ma. She's big.

Henry Fonda is still staring at me. I've swallowed my tongue; there's nothing there.

He sneers. I see it—the corner of his mouth. And, beside me, I hear my da breathe out. He's relieved. He thinks it's over—I can't stand up to the Garda and we can all go home. The cop starts to turn again, away from me. I can see Ms. Nigeria. She's looking down the corridor at her ma and da. I'm losing my chance.

But, bang on time, my tongue's back. It climbs back up from my stomach.

"Eh."

The cop stops. I speak.

"What's your name, by the way?"

I hear him—he kind of whispers.

"What?"

It doesn't look too bad there on the page, just the one word, like. But you'd want to have heard it. I hold on to my tongue; I don't let it escape. I ask him again.

"What's your name?"

I hear my da.

"Son…"

I ignore him—I have to.

The cop walks up nearer to me. He's not Henry Fonda now. He's become Dennis Hopper. I kind of miss Henry.

"Why?" he says.

"Cos I'm going to report you."

I can nearly see the words, going in an arc through the air, from my mouth to the space between his eyes, where his eyebrows join together.

He doesn't go pale. He doesn't fall on his knees and beg for mercy. It's a pity.

The room is frozen, everyone in it. It's, like, one big gasp. And Ms. Nigeria—you should see her eyes. They're huge and lit, and they're looking at me. Her da is coming toward us. Her ma is right behind him.

But back to the cop. He's coming straight at—

Sorry for interrupting my own story here—but all this actually happened. I just want you to know that.

Anyway. He's coming straight at me.

Remember the sweets? They're back in my mouth, the taste, the sugar and that.

"Report me for what?"

That's the cop.

And listen to this.

"For using racist language intended to inflict hurt on a member of an ethnic minority," I say.

And I nod at Ms. Nigeria.

"Her."

He doesn't say anything. Her da is right behind him now.

"And for making me put up my hoodie in front of the camera," I say.

I probably shouldn't have mentioned the hoodie. I can see it on her face: she's confused. The Fed is still looking at me and he's not confused at all. But there's no stopping me now. I'm starring in my own film. *I'm* Henry Fonda.

"I'll probably let you away with the hoodie," I say. "But not the racism."

"You're threatening me?" says the Fed.

"No, he's not," says Ms. Nigeria.

"No, I'm not," I agree.

But—funny—I'm a little bit annoyed. I mean, I love her voice and the way she talks and that. But this is between me and the Fed, so I wish she'd just shut up for a bit and, like, admire me—just for a minute. Is that too much to ask?

Anyway.

"I just want to know your name," I tell the Fed—before she does.

Her da's arrived and he looks the business. His suit is blue and serious looking. But the really serious thing about him is his face. He's the most serious-looking man I've ever seen. I'd say Ireland's overall seriousness went up at least 25 percent the day he got here from Nigeria. Like, the situation was pretty serious before he came into the station. But now—Jaysis—it's an international crisis. I can tell from the heads on the cops: they wish they were in sunny Baghdad. And he hasn't even spoken yet.

But now he does.

CHAPTER EIGHT

"What exactly is the problem here?" says Ms. Nigeria's da.

His voice takes over the room, and the station, and the street—the dogs bark in Coolock and Clondalkin. He's huge. He's like a whole African country, Uganda or somewhere, that just stood up one day and put on a suit. Like, he's massive and so is his voice.

And so is his wife—you should see her. If he's the country, she's the country's biggest lake or something.

Back to Ms. Nigeria's da. It's not that he's actually massive. He just seems like that. Impressive—that's a better word. Or frightening—that's another one.

I look across at Ms. Nigeria. She doesn't look frightened. And she doesn't look impressed.

"I texted you *ages* ago," she says.

"One minute, young lady," he says, and he stops—he drops anchor beside the plainclothes Fed.

"I am—Name Omitted," he says. "This is my wife. You have incarcerated our daughter. Why?"

The Fed is trying to make himself taller. He's up on his toes.

"Shoplifting," he says.

"Ridiculous," says her da.

My da speaks now.

"I don't suppose there's a back way out."

He kind of whispers. I think he's messing.

"It is a quite legitimate business venture," Ms. Nigeria's da tells the Fed, and the rest of Dublin. "Conducted in concert with her schoolfellows."

"It looked very like shoplifting," says the Fed, "from our perspective."

You can tell. He's trying to talk like her da. But it's not working. "Perspective" comes out like he's not all that certain what it means.

Anyway, it goes on like this for a while, the two of them throwing the dictionaries. And it gets a bit boring. I look at not-Superman. He's recovered, more or less. He knows he's not going to Guantanamo Bay and they won't be painting his wheelchair orange. His brother's okay too. The color is back in his cheeks—whatever that means.

I look at the plainclothes Fed. He looks a bit out of it. Ms. Nigeria's da is still giving it to him; he's demanding a tribunal into the circumstances of his daughter's arrest—I think. I bet I could go over and just happy-slap the Fed, lift my arm and clothesline the bollix. I could film it on my phone and put it up on Bebo when I get home.

But I don't. It's not my style. And my phone's gone dead.

I look at Ms. Nigeria. She's standing beside her ma.

My granda's an alco and he once told me that if I wanted to know what my girlfriend was going to look like when she got older I should take a good look at her ma. Like, I was only about six when he told me and I was trying to stop him from falling down the stairs but, even so, it had sounded kind of cool.

So, now's my chance.

She's there with her ma.

Maybe she's adopted.

But I don't really think that. I'm still in love and a bit—I don't know—hyper. Like, I've been arrested and interrogated. I've been accused and framed. I've stood up to the cops and accused them of racism and frame-ation, or whatever it's called. I'm like your man coming out of the court at the end *In the Name of the Father*: "I am an inno-cent mon!" Except for the sweets. And, just to remind you—all this happened in about half an hour.

And, I have to admit, her ma's lovely too. Big and all. Black-big has a lot more going for it than white-big—in my opinion, like. You should see her hair. It's amazing—it's like hundreds of snakes curled up on her head. It's not a ma's hair-style at all.

Anyway. We all leave together. We charge out of the cop shop. "I am an inno-cent mon!" And we follow Ms. Nigeria's da. All of us. I don't know why. We don't seem to have a choice. My da catches up with him, and they're chatting away. We follow them back over the bridge at Tara Street. The wind is knocking us all over the shop.

I was going to say a lot more about stereotyping and racism and that. I was kind of angry when I started. I don't know what happened. Maybe it's this. By the time we get over the bridge and we're going past Liberty Hall, she's holding my hand. I think she's my girlfriend. Ms. Nigeria, like—not her ma. But, like I said, it's pretty windy. Maybe she's afraid it'll pick her up and throw her in the Liffey, so she's hanging on to me. But I don't think so. I think I'm her fella. So, like—nice one. We'll see how it goes.

I NEVER WANTED TO BE a criminal until I was one. And then, for a while, I couldn't imagine wanting to be anything else.

I was seventeen when Dad got out of prison for the second time. Aunt Fay didn't want me to go back to him. "Stay," she told me, fanning out community college brochures on the formica table. "Finish your school."

For two years, she and Uncle Mitch had been great—everything open-door, come and go, free access to the fridge, a place of my own in the basement. Mitch worked at the seed company, and Fay baked bread and fried doughnuts at Safeway. They liked to drink beer on the couch or head down to the Mirage to play pool and listen to the same songs on the jukebox.

Then Fay woke up New Year's Day with a huge bruise on her hip that she couldn't remember how she got. It was spectacular—a saddle around her side, back, and stomach, purple-blue and wavy on the edges, yellow and red in the middle.

Mitch said, "Search me."

That morning I'd woken up before everybody else, gotten a box of Count Chocula, and sat on the couch with the TV on, eating by the handful in my underwear and T-shirt. Fay came out at noon, dream-logged and slow. She was poking at her side and wincing when she saw me. She stood in the frame of the hall, and her guilty look made me ashamed.

After that, Fay always wanted to know where I was going and how I was doing in school. She quit drinking. She cut her hair short. When Dad's release date started getting close, she talked to me about staying put and finishing school, about stability, the importance of education.

"They've got all kinds of things," she said one night, turning the glossy pages. "You can train for all kinds of good jobs."

She wore her Safeway smock and smelled of fryer grease. She flipped the pages on programs to become a diesel mechanic, a licensed practical nurse, a computer programmer. I looked at the brochures, with the smiling students taking a temperature or probing a truck engine, and pictured myself in that world, getting smarter and earning money, falling in love and living in a house like a real person. Fay was so hung with expectation that I told her okay, but I never thought we were talking about anything real. I figured her for two or three months of the straight and narrow until something glassy showed in her eyes again.

Dad wore the same thing coming out he wore going in: jeans, snap-button shirt, cowboy boots. His clothes seemed hangy and big, like he'd shrunk inside them, and his sideburns were turning gray.

We drove to Boise to pick him up in his own car, the slouching, soft-shocked Pontiac. Mitch drove, guiding us in and out of the passing lane, and Fay talked and talked. I stretched my legs out on the back seat, sick with nerves, but then we saw him and he was just Dad, and he hugged me and joked around and called me kiddo.

"You're getting *huge,*" he said, like he hadn't seen me two months before. He and Fay and Mitch all laughed at this, my unbelievable growth. Fay had us stand back-to-back and said I had him by an inch. "Stop it already," he said.

In the car Fay talked about where to go for lunch. Dad said he'd heard about a good Basque place from one of the guys in his anger management sessions.

"Embezzler," he said, and laughed. "Angry embezzler."

We ate lamb stew and chorizo and spicy potatoes and thick soup, drinking it all down with red wine. Dad ate two of everything, wiped his bread around the curve of his bowl and smiled while he chewed. Afterward we went to the park by the river and Dad kneeled down in the cold grass and ran his hands over it, put his face down and breathed it in, and then he lay on it, face down. He turned over on his back, eyes closed, smiling.

On the way home he sprawled out on the seat beside me, so relaxed he seemed ready to come apart completely.

"Must be great to be out," I said.

"It's all right," he said, opening his eyes and looking away.

Months later we picked up the man in the tan suit at the diner. We drove him into the desert. He was trying to get home to see his daughter in Boise. He'd left her and her mother years ago, left and never went back. He was afraid she'd never forgive him.

"Nothing more important than family," Dad said. "She's got to realize that."

I had no friends then. Not one. I knew people, and I'd had friendships here and there, but something always broke them up. Mostly we'd just gradually stop being friends, the way we'd gradually started. When my seventeenth birthday came, a couple months before Dad got out, Mitch, Fay, and I went to Café Olé in Twin Falls, where the waiters come out and sing and put a sombrero on you and take a Polaroid. Fay told me I could bring a friend, but I couldn't think of anyone. We'd lived in Gooding all our lives.

In the picture, Fay is poised, arm around my shoulder. Mitch looks out of the frame. My face is hidden by the shadow of the sombrero. If you saw it, you'd think: mother, father, son.

On the way home from Boise that first day, Fay worked herself up and turned around and told Dad she thought I should stay with her and Mitch, at least until I finished school.

Dad tipped his head—like, *maybe*—and chewed the inside of his lip.

Fay said it would just be for stability, so I could get through classes without disruption. I was three months from graduation. She told him about the community college, the mechanics program, the bright future and common sense.

"Well," he said finally, "I guess I just always figured I'd have my boy with me."

My blood raced. Nobody spoke for the longest time.

"You're not exactly set up to be a parent right now, Reed," Fay said. "Forgive my saying."

Mitch said, "Fay."

Dad didn't say anything. I held my breath, afraid I'd be asked to decide.

The man in the tan suit said he was trying to get to Boise to see his daughter. He hadn't seen her in twelve years. She was flying in from Oregon. He smelled like the front part of a department store, glass cases and glass bottles, chemical sweet. He'd moved to Idaho and taken another job and bought a house and met another woman.

"Like that other life hadn't ever been," he said.

Dad drove us down the freeway. He kept smiling at the man, tapping his hands on the steering wheel. I sat with my legs out on the back seat. We'd put our last seven dollars into the gas tank.

The man told us bits at a time. He was driving to Boise from Twin Falls, going to pick up his daughter at the airport, when he broke down. The mechanic needed a day to get the part, but that airplane from Oregon was on its way.

My father kept looking at me, his icy green eyes framed in the rearview mirror. He might have been mad at me, still. Or trying to communicate something. But there was nothing that perfect between us, no secret eye language of family.

The muscle beneath his left eye quivered, and he placed a finger on it, held it in place until it stopped.

When I was eleven, I watched Dad drag a teenager from his car in the parking lot at the swimming pool, shouting so loud a lifeguard came out to break it up.

"I'm going to kick your ass up between your shoulder blades," Dad shouted as he backed away. "You'll have to take off your shirt to take a shit."

The guy had been taunting me and Bucky Torr, a neighbor kid who'd come swimming with me. We were standing in our wet suits, wrapped in towels, on the lawn outside the pool. He'd called us pussies, dared us to grab the tits of the girls nearby. Bucky was about to cry, and when Dad pulled up and asked him what was wrong, he told him.

Watching my father looking at us over his elbow on the open car window I could see it all happening, even though I couldn't tell you what it was. Something widened in his pupils and his nostrils. His face filled with blood. Then the door was swinging at us and we jumped out of the way.

Dad rented us an apartment downtown, above the Lincoln Inn. He got a job milking and lost it three days later, when the owner found out he'd been in prison. The guy said if Dad had only been honest, he might have kept him on.

"No way," Dad told me.

He started working the swing shift at Quik Mart, coming home afterward and telling me to go to bed. He asked about school, tried to keep the fridge full. He seemed nervous and dry-mouthed all the time. It was almost two weeks before they let him go.

He went to visit his parole officer in Twin Falls, and came back agitated.

"Like I haven't already had two jobs," he said. "Like I'm just sitting here."

He started staying out later, and then he vanished for two days. I stayed home, skipping school and waiting. I thought maybe I was already alone and just didn't know it yet, like he'd crashed that Pontiac and died but nobody knew to find me and tell me. I thought if that was true maybe I'd just stay still forever, inside the gray bubble of those days, and stop pretending there were other people for me.

He came back with a little money, said he'd found work roofing in Idaho Falls and meant to call, etc. We went downstairs for burgers. He had three beers with dinner, and he stayed in the bar when I came up and went to sleep.

The next morning, a Thursday, I walked down the hall and saw Dad sprawled out on his mattress, on top of the covers in his clothes. Everything was gray-lit and quiet. I walked back down the hall and climbed into bed.

The day we met the man in the tan suit, we were out of money, angry, quiet. In a diner with vinyl seats, looking out a plate glass window onto the Snake River. The man came in, looked around, walked over, and offered to pay us for a ride to Boise.

"What do you think—twenty bucks?" he asked. "Thirty?"

He wore a tie, neat as a banker. He carried a deep maroon briefcase. He smelled nicer than men I knew, and his eyes seemed loose and watery on his face. I could probably remember his name if I had to. It was just him and us in there, not counting the waitress and the cook.

"We're going that way," Dad said. "Buy our coffee and we'll call it good."

I scooted over and the man sat down.

"I've got money," he said. He took a worn envelope from his briefcase, thick with bills, and slid out a single twenty.

Dad wouldn't hear of it. He never looked at the money, but he seemed like he was smelling it or tasting it. A blush high on his cheeks, and a spasm under one eye.

When Dad's parole officer knocked, announcing himself from the hallway—"Reed? It's Barrett Rudman. Open up"—I was both surprised and not, because some part of fearing is expecting. Dad motioned me into the bedroom and closed the door behind me.

I heard the man say he'd had a report that Dad had been drinking in a bar. Dad asked who'd said that, and the man said it didn't matter, was it true, and Dad said no.

"If it is, I don't have to tell you what that means," the man said.

Dad said he hadn't been in a bar since his parole. He said he'd been working construction jobs, day work, and gave the name of a contractor he could check with. He said he spent a lot of time with me, who lived with his Aunt Fay and Uncle Mitch.

He was an excellent liar. Really good. But it sounded like the parole officer didn't believe him. He told Dad to be careful. He said, "I'll be stopping by again."

Dad said fine, good, look forward to it. After the man left, Dad said, "That fucking Fay," and he went into the kitchen, opening and closing cupboards, slamming things, and then again, "That goddamned fucking Fay."

* * *

Dad disappeared again. For two days I went back to thinking he'd died without me knowing, or some other bad thing, but by the third day, when the food ran out, I knew he'd just left and wouldn't ever be back, and that Fay had been right all along.

That afternoon I walked to her house. They were both at work. I walked through the back door and went right to the box of Quaker Oats in the cupboard, where Fay hid her spending money. Thirty-four bucks. I went through the cupboards and the drawers. In the hallway closet, I grabbed Mitch's binoculars. In the bedroom, I took Fay's Walkman and some jewelry that probably wasn't worth a thing. I found sixty bucks hidden under some socks in Mitch's drawer.

I walked around, looking for something else worth taking, but everything seemed too cheap or too big or too worn out. On the fridge Fay had the picture of us at Café Olé, and another one of her and me, hung by magnets. I wanted to do more, something to show I'd been here, to say hello and fuck you, to say none of you get me now, but I couldn't think of a single other thing.

At the grocery story I bought eggs, ham, and bread. I ate the same kind of sandwich four meals straight. Dusk drifted through the apartment all the time. It felt like I might never have to see another person. I kept the blinds down. I looked over the jobs in the *Gooding County Leader* and wondered how you even tried to get one.

It was noon and Dad was drunk when he came back, wobbly and smiling to himself.

"Hey, kiddo," he said when he walked in.

I didn't answer.

"Come on, now," he said, slumping onto the couch and throwing an arm around me. "Don't be like that. I found a little work."

I watched the TV.

"In Boise. Hanging drywall."

When I didn't answer, his smile fell. He took his arm back and went into the kitchen, banging around until he came back with a bottle of Jack Daniel's and a glass. He poured himself about six fingers. He watched me steadily between gulps. I fixed my eyes on the TV screen.

"Fine," he said, and carried his glass back into the kitchen. When he came back, he said, "Hey," and threw his car keys at me.

"Come on," he said. "You're driving."

* * *

I drove us to the outskirts of town, and he had me park on the shoulder, across the street from a gravel cul-de-sac rimmed with Boise Cascade homes stamped from the same blueprint. A blue one, a brown one, a yellow one. Windows all dark. People out living. He shushed me when I started to speak, and we sat there for twenty minutes.

Then Dad rubbed his hands on his jeans like he was trying to get feeling back in his fingers. He said, "I want you to promise me you'll never tell anyone about this." He said, "You've got to listen to everything. Listen, listen, listen. Ask yourself what every sound is." He said, "We run at the first sign of trouble. There's plenty of time if you don't wait for things to get worse."

We walked down the lane, swishing through ditch weeds to avoid the noisy gravel, and came to a small house with a big fence toward the only neighbor. No dog barked. We circled behind and watched the back door.

He said, "Usually, the back door's best. I bet you a hundred bucks that back door's open, and if it's not, the next twenty-five will be." He said, "When you get in, stand absolutely still for twenty or thirty seconds. Listen."

We were going in there. I never had a doubt. I was high on it.

The man in the tan suit kept thanking us. I watched Dad's eyes in the mirror and wondered what we were doing. The money radiated through the car.

"A lot of people wouldn't just help a stranger like this," the man said. "Not like they used to."

"Don't give it another thought," Dad said.

We'd have to work for days to fill an envelope like that.

"For all you know, I could be a dangerous man. On the lam."

"You don't seem the type," Dad said, eyes in the mirror.

"Some kind of scumbag," the man said.

The color climbed Dad's neck.

Inside that first house, Dad motioned for me to stand still in the kitchen and watch him. He walked to drawers and opened them slowly. In one, he found a checkbook, which he lifted and pointed to, nodding and smiling. He put it back. He walked into the living room, looking back at me every so often, lifting objects and replacing them, opening doors, nudging things on the tables, showing me how silently he could move through absent lives. He put everything back, that time. He'd never steal anything that close to home.

Except, as we left, he picked up a cookie jar from the counter and tucked it under his arm. It was a ceramic French pig. You took off its beret to get at the cookies. We ate some in the car on the way back home. Store-bought.

Dad put the pig in the center of the kitchen table, and we ate all the cookies in two days. That jar sat there for three months, though it never held another cookie. It was where we kept the money. We'd take off in the Pontiac for a week to the podunk Mormon towns around Salt Lake, come back with checkbooks and new clothes and rolls of cash. We'd head over to Helena and come back with a trunk-load of shotguns to pawn.

The cookie jar was always full. Dad would buy us beer and we'd get drunk. He'd coach me on the finer points. We played cards and ate steak four times a week. I never got up in the morning, and never worried about getting to bed. I never had a moral qualm, I'm sorry to say. It was too much damn fun. Too much adrenaline and freedom. Me and my dad, money in the pig, nowhere to be.

We were sitting on the couch after dusting off a twelve-pack one night when he told me my hairline was receding. I reached up to feel it.

"No," I said.

"Yes sir," he said. "It's starting."

Dad had a widow's peak, an isthmus of hair with deep recessions at the temples. I began checking my forehead carefully in the mirror, and some days I thought he was right and some days I thought he was wrong. I liked the thought of it at first, the idea that there might be some physical evidence connecting us. Then it started seeming like the start of something unstoppable.

At some point Dad went to the pig and found six dollars. He crashed into my bedroom and started shoving things around on my dresser.

"What happened to all the money?" he said.

I was in bed, waking up. He opened the drawers, clawed through my clothes.

"You took some out," he said.

"Knock it off," I said. "There's no money in there. I might have a few bucks in my pants pocket, but that's it."

He picked up my pants and pulled out three crumpled ones. His eyes slid around in his twitchy face.

"Dad, come on."

He left for the rest of the day. That night he sat next to me on the couch and slapped me on the knee a couple times. He said we'd take off for Boise in the morning to fill up the pig.

"Hey, kiddo, I'm sorry about earlier. I was just surprised, is all."

I kept looking at the TV.

"Come on, Zach. You know I love you."

The next day we met the man in the tan suit and gave him a ride and learned all about his failed first life and his happy second life and how he planned to make things right and how he hoped his daughter could forgive him.

She was nineteen. Someone had cut out her wedding announcement and sent it to him. When he saw it, he tracked her down and called her. Bought her a plane ticket.

"I left them in my dark days," he said. "I left them all alone. I'm afraid she'll never forgive me."

We were driving on the freeway to Boise, windows down, the sweet, dusty odor of hay on the rushing air. Dad's gun in a bag at my feet. We turned off at Mountain Home. Dad told the man he had to swing by a friend's place, and then he drove deep into the desert, following county roads until they turned to gravel. He found a place beside a stand of trees.

"Got to see a man about a horse," he said, and then he yawned big, stretched his arms wide, and while the man looked outside, unafraid, Dad dropped his right arm, looked at me in the back seat like he was sending a message, and pointed at the bag sitting on the floor beside me.

I thought it was a big mistake, but I had no language for that.

Dad said, "Look for cash. Things that are small and valuable. Jewelry. Some kinds of knives. Binoculars." He said, "Don't shit where you eat. My rule is nothing closer than one hundred miles from home." He said, "Sometimes I think this is a mistake, what we're doing." He said, "Now you try it." He said, "Just squeeze." He said, "Sometimes I think this is the best life ever. I think of those people sound asleep right now, alarm clocks and ties and shit, and I think if you can just keep this going, it's the luckiest thing ever." He said, "If your mother could see this, God rest her, I'd catch hell." He said, "You know I love you, kiddo." He said, "Sir, we're gonna have to take that briefcase." He said, "All right now, sir, hand over that case or my boy will shoot you." He said, "We won't have any choice." He said, "Jesus Christ, Zach. Hold it like you mean it."

THEY WERE IN MAINE when it seemed Hurricane Wilma might hit land in Key West. Casey's husband, Paul, was a painter whose canvases contained shapes that looked like the eye of a hurricane; maybe he'd always been prescient. They had no children, but were inordinately fond of their dog, and often drove between the places they lived (Maine, Virginia, and Florida), so the dog would not have to be put in a cage on an airplane.

2005 was proving to be a bad year for hurricanes, so they had lingered in Maine, but today was the day Casey felt she had to call the travel agent. She still used a travel agent because when plans had to change—as they would increasingly, with glaciers melting and seas turning into hot tubs—it was consoling to be able to rearrange things with a real human being. Casey had also just gotten a bit of good news, which would simplify things: Bruce, the neighbor's son, would be driving south, so Casey had arranged for him to drive Folly as far as Atlanta (she and Paul would fly), where they'd rendezvous at a restaurant owned by one of the Spice Girls (Bruce's idea), after which she and Paul and the dog would continue in a rented car to Key West.

"That should work out well," the travel agent said. "Eventually this hurricane will decide where it's going! So let's see... I route you first to Atlanta." Casey thought that if she told the travel agent she needed to rendezvous with the Magi, the woman would have asked where, and on what date.

Casey added quietly, in case Paul was listening: "Paul doesn't want to put the dog on a plane."

The travel agent lowered her voice, too: "I know *exactly,* because I'm that way about Mr. Bones."

Mr. Bones was the sleek black cat with two raindrops of white on one ear, who watched the travel agent work, peering from his perch behind an enormous philodendron on top of a bookshelf.

"Men!" the travel agent said. "All men but Mama's darling, Mr. Bones."

True to her word, the travel agent was not upset when Casey called the next day to say they would like to fly directly into Key West. For a sum, the neighbor's boy would drive Folly right to their door in Key West, get there before them, and use Casey's spare key, then wait for them to arrive. He would do this because: (1) the house was safe, windows boarded up by the caretaker, and (2) he had met a girl who would be starting a job as a barista on a huge yacht coming from Providence, R.I., to dock at Key West, and he and she could do depraved things in the house for days before Paul and Casey arrived. The only problem might be the highway: they were threatening to close Route 1 south of Miami. Anyone's getting to Key West might depend on Wilma changing course: right now, the hurricane was spinning like a cosmically swirling finger-to-the-ear, indicating: *The person who has just passed by is completely crazy.*

Well, said the travel agent, why not assume the best? They could always find an alternative if need be. She booked them on Delta: mileage upgrades to first class, aisle and window-seat preferences, at 11:30 a.m. She said: "No problem. This is my caffeine. I mainline travel plans. That's what I do."

The travel plans of others are not interesting, though for those involved, they are completely preoccupying. It's generally understood that other people will not keep track of your travel plans, nor you theirs.

But weather scrambles the best-laid plans, and Casey and Paul and the travel agent (who deserves a name: Judy Brackett) were sent into turnaround by Hurricane Wilma. What the dog came to see in the Key West house will only be related briefly because (1) it happened mostly in the dark and (2) dogs go about their business, whatever the circumstances. The dog did not care that Bruce and the girl drank scotch and watered the bottle; that they sat in the bathtub shaping piles of bubbles into Santa beards; that Bruce strutted around wearing one of Casey's La Perla camisoles, while the girl put on Paul's swim trunks, so big they made her look like a two-tentacled man-o'-war. The dog had minimal interest in their doing it on the granite kitchen counter, Bruce wincing as he licked key-lime juice he'd squeezed onto her breasts. Aprés sex, they raced into a windstorm on the back deck, holding big fronds that had blown off a palm like fans in a vaudeville act, peeking through them coyly.

The weather got worse, the sky darkened, only to be ripped apart by brightness. The police had twice ridden through the streets with bullhorns, ordering immediate evacuation. The dog retreated to his cushion and curled up. On the deck, defying wind and rain, the two naked lovers leaped and shrieked, as the wind ripped orchids from their mossy tree nests to shoot past them like prettily colored rockets. Her palm frond went airborne, though she'd thought she had a Mary Poppins grip on it. So did somebody's laundry: a white shirt slammed into the big tree in the backyard and stayed there, like a poultice on a sore. The rain was painful, it came down so hard. She saw welts on her body when they rushed inside, Bruce steadying himself to close the shuttered doors to the deck just as the lights flickered and went out. The noise of the storm numbed their ears. He had seen a candle somewhere. The bathroom! That was where—a giant candle surrounded by shells and items the owners must have found amusing: little plastic mermaids; a (as best he could make out) miniature robotic cheetah. But matches, matches... too utilitarian for these people, not in drawers, not anywhere. The next crash sounded like two cars hitting, head-on, though he thought it also might have been thunder. Matches! In a bowl with keys and pens. He struck one to see the girl curled on the cushion behind the dog, clinging to her fur life raft. The wick of the candle caught fire, and he saw as it made light that he'd cut his hip, running from the back deck.

"What if the wind rips the boards off?" the girl said. (She would never be a barista, now: the OUR TOMORROW'S PARTIES had turned back toward Providence two days earlier.) He could not hear her, though, because the dog barked: three high-pitched yelps. She squinted to see him: this naked, gangly man fussing with a candle was certainly not her tall, Jagger-lipped former fiancé—and she suddenly knew that the roof would blow off, while this man with his skinny butt, bleeding… no, no, *wrong, wrong, wrong,* she thought, just before everything was colorized into a weirdly irradiated, yellowy darkness that couldn't be squinted away. She saw the same deeper color inside her eyelids. Color and sound became the same thing: blinding, deafening. She stayed where she was, arm thrown over the dog, touching her ears to see if they'd collapsed and become concave, pretending Folly needed comfort. Outside, something thudded down. It sounded like a tree dropping on a drum. Car alarms beeped. She was afraid to move. Something (the candle had gone out; he'd relit the candle) hit the house right behind where she and the dog lay, the cushion she would never in a million years have plunked down on, except that her ringing ears made her dizzy. He had cut his hip. She was wondering whether he would ever crouch to comfort her. As something else crashed outside, the dog raised its head and shuddered a deep breath, sending saliva across her cheek. "Eww!" she screamed, scrambling to stand. The candle wick was no good: the flame kept dying. Skinnyman stood with his back to her, trying to peek out the window where a sliver of light came in between the glass and the board. What did he find so interesting? Rain pelted the roof. She'd have to shout to be heard, and she didn't have the strength. She'd had too much to drink earlier. The dog stood and moved toward a chair, clawing his way under. Outside, someone screamed and was joined by other voices that sounded like the Vienna Boys' Choir in hell, finally drowned out by an ambulance siren. She had a headache, a toothache (she explored with her tongue), her lips felt frozen. She hated him—absolutely hated Skinnyman, and whoever the rich people were who owned this house that seemed about to blow away. Here she was in Hurricane Wilma, the hurricane she'd *told* him wasn't going to blow over. She stood, feeling the room constrict. The house was a noisy cocktail shaker, and she was a little ice cube, bobbing.

Judy Brackett's call was the first to get through. After the storm blew over (the crazy girl locked in the bathroom), he heard the first bars of "I Love a Parade" on his cell phone, and flipped it open to say: "Hullo?"

His clothes stank, he realized when he lifted his arm. He had just finished eating a plate of red beans. Was the girl punishing him for something he'd done? What the hell was wrong with girls? What was it with them, that they wouldn't speak? He and the dog had bonded, at least. It raised its snout with concern to the place where he'd skinned himself, sniffing delicately. He'd unscrewed the plywood on the little kitchen window. There was no longer a roof on the garage. A palm tree was lying on the people's car roof, their—it looked to be—little black Mercedes. "Okay, never eat again, see if I care," he called. Had she killed herself in there? Why was he bothering to listen to static over the phone? "Hullo?" he said one more time, angrily. The response was: "Wilma... sc... terday... tomorrow... sczzzzzzzz. Hello?"

He said loudly, no idea who it was: "Mom?"

"Sczzzzzzzzzz Brackett sczzzzzzzzz."

"What?"

"Their travel agent" came through loud and clear. He jerked the phone away from his ear. He hadn't heard another voice for a long time.

"Their house sczzzzzzzzzz? Lost scccczzzzzz control tower, airport?"

"The house is still here. The dog's fine," he said. He thought the voice must have been trying to ask those things.

"Sczzzzzzzzzzzzzzzzzz."

"Yeah, their car had some damage. Can you hear me? Actually a tree fell on their car."

The voice repeated, as if from a great distance: "I'm their travel agent."

"Well, that's good," he said, and immediately felt foolish, though why should he have felt foolish?

"Sczzzzzzzzzzzzz, port closed?"

"I don't—I haven't gone out of the house," he said. He didn't think taking the dog into the backyard to pee counted. There was furniture in the pool of the house next door, and he could see a shape he thought was a drowned cat. When last he checked the dog had been looking glum, keeping a vigil, lying against the locked bathroom door. He had fed the dog a can of beans while he ate his.

"Airport's closed," the voice said. "They can't get there. What damage sczzzzzzzzzz? Sczzzzzzz."

"I'm fine. There's some damage—a tree fucked up the car." He didn't think the other person could hear much of what he said. It was a she. Had she said she was a travel agent? Was a travel agent trying to get him out? He could just imagine what had happened to his car. He sighed deeply and felt a sharp pain beneath his ribs. The dog wasn't that light; he shouldn't have picked it up, earlier, just because it was quivering.

A man had jumped into the pool next door, and was screaming.

Two days after the Key West airport opened, Casey and Paul stepped onto the tarmac. At the end of the runway were flooded police cars, drowned by a tidal surge, waiting to be hauled away. They took in everything at once, then averted their eyes, as if they were at a funeral. People were weeping in the airport; they came to meet their friends and relatives in pajamas with nylon jackets thrown on top, as if they'd left the hospital for a brief time, to get their affairs in order. Everyone seemed to need something, but to be unable to articulate that need. There was a line of people waiting at the water fountain, but they all moved away when one of the pilots passed by and told them not to drink the water.

Outside, it looked like winter. It had from the air, too. Everything brown, leafless.

She thought that she should not have let Bruce take the dog. She understood from the travel agent that Folly was fine, but still: it had been stupid of her to delegate such responsibility.

She looked at Paul. She felt that they were not so much walking as drifting. People around them in the airprot spoke in hushed voices. No one sat behind any of the car rental stands. A broken window was crisscrossed with duct tape. The broken glass looked like the spider veins on her thighs, Casey thought miserably. Outside, they were surprised to see several cabs. A man in a baseball cap, shorts, and a white T-shirt advertising One-To-One held a hand-lettered sign with the name of one of the big hotels. He stood beside a Ford Explorer with a severely dented hood. She had the bad feeling that something—if not the dog, something—bad awaited them. And this had been their sanctuary! The place she'd felt most free, the place where she could decorate with a sense of humor, put a plastic flamingo near the pool, and everyone would understand she was kidding. The place where she could forget about makeup, put on a floppy hat, wear flip-flops to the Tropic Cinema.

They got in a pink Flamingo taxi and the driver set off, answering questions but volunteering little. She saw piles of broken fences. Had there been that many fences? Everything looked so much smaller; with the fences down, you could see how little land there was separating houses. The hurricane had demystified everything: gates had been ripped away, so that they were no longer portals to private gardens with walls of orchids, to the tantalizingly unknown. Houses stood bare, without landscaping, without little Buddha statues guarding pansies, fountains toppled, Neptune beheaded. No flashes of color caught your eye: no spills of bougainvillea; no fuchsia borders of impatiens; the only color provided by clothing in the street, already drying as if it had been washed, wrung out, and left twisted on the ground. Sometimes there was a bit of color that you soon realized was rotting food. Paul gave thanks that they lived in Old Town, on the highest point of the island, where there had not been so much flooding. He noticed driftwood, broken bicycles, spilled garbage that out-Dali'd Dali. The eerie quiet... it was too quiet. He said, for the tenth time that day: "The dog is fine."

The sky was acid blue, tinged bilious yellow. She had never seen such a sky in Key West.

Only a little way from the airport exit the road was cluttered with refrigerators and stoves, all sorts of appliances, ruined furniture in piles. Plywood hung off buildings. Abandoned cars sat crookedly at the side of the road; one was on its side, and bicycles had drifted around it like maggots. Trees were down everywhere. Sand had washed thickly across the road. There was only one lane, though it was going in the direction they wanted to go. He took her hand. She squeezed. The lights weren't working at the intersection, and the driver inched forward, looking left and right before flooring it across Roosevelt Boulevard. "It's worse than we were told," Paul said. The cab driver answered: "My brother's boat sank. Lived on the boat until I got married."

They rode in silence. Her hand felt strange—little and strange—in his. Everything was wrecked: boats sunk near their moorings; upended cars become metallic totem poles, grills grinning crookedly. The cab driver said something, but he was only muttering to himself. Real estate prices were sure to fall. Wilma would mark the end of that madness. Their street was barricaded. The cab let them off at the corner.

The traveler's palm was gone. There was a big hole where it had been, muddily cradling a broken Yoda and a dead chicken. She looked up and saw, on the front porch of the second story, her beloved dog sitting with a young man she wouldn't have recognized if she'd passed him on the street, grizzly-bearded, bare-chested, feet on the railing, a can of Coke next to his foot. Though she could see Folly's brown shape, he did not see her. He sat like a stone dog, staring straight ahead, close to the young man's chair, which was not a chair they owned. It would turn out that he had removed it from the street so cars could pass. It had sat there for days, and then—because their porch furniture had all been ruined when it had blown to the ground—he'd lugged the heavy chair into the house and used it to sit on the porch, where he had a better view of the devastation.

He'd been good to their dog. They'd never know a girl had even been in the place. She had left without a word: a day and night locked in the bathroom, then the door opened and she walked right past, not looking at him, saying nothing, and out the front door he'd removed the plywood from that morning. Not long after that the caretaker had come around to turn on the generator. The refrigerator had clunked on: cold Coke! The caretaker had lost his trailer; he didn't know where to go. His wife worked at the hospital, but the fire chief refused to let the hospital staff put up tents in the parking lot. Of course he didn't dare ask the man to pry off all the wood he'd nailed in the windows. They'd stood there, slick with sweat, hands at their sides as if they'd just finished a fight neither had won. It had been a long time since he'd seen a man crying. While these thoughts went through his mind, Casey and Paul had nearly reached the house, Paul with a shoulder bag, pulling a suitcase, she with a big purse slung over her shoulder.

Bruce was exhausted; since Wilma'd passed over, he just couldn't sleep. Bravo that these people had stayed married for however many years they'd stayed married. Hurricanes were named for women, and that seemed right. Oh, sure, now they had to be named for men, too, everybody had to be dragged in for the sake of equality, so hurricanes could be given New Age names, they could be… hell, they could be named for drugs: Hurricane Ambien. He was lucky his car hadn't been damaged. Now he could go back to his parents and try to play the hurricane card into a reason for his father to send him to graduate school, which sucked a lot less than having to get a job.

"Come back here, you sonofabitch," a woman screamed from the doorway diagonally across the street. A cat ran from behind her, into the yard. A man looking dazed, wearing shorts and a white T-shirt, stalked into his front lawn with a chain-saw and began cutting up the tree that had fallen across the path. The cat had disap-peared. The woman continued to scream, but Bruce couldn't hear what she said.

Casey glanced in the woman's direction, then bent to shake a rock out of her shoe. Who were these tenants, who rented the house that had been falling into the ground before the hurricane? So many of their friends lived elsewhere, and only came to Key West in season, when the danger of hurricanes had passed. Would they even come from D.C. this year? How did they ever come to rent to such peo-ple, the man raising the chainsaw to the sky every few seconds, jabbing in the direction of the sky, the woman standing in her underwear in the doorway, scream-ing? Paul paid no attention to them, and lent her his arm. The chainsaw roared. There was food decaying in gutters. Ears of corn… when did you see ears of corn in Key West? A crazy woman strolled by, singing a cracked version of "Amazing Grace" and pushing a cart full of beer bottles. Casey bent again to shake another pebble from her shoe. They had been walking on the sidewalk through drifts of gravel and dirt, dotted with ears of corn, smashed glass, and another neighbor's decapitated flamingo mailbox.

Earlier that afternoon, the strangest thing had happened. Bruce had gone down-stairs when he'd heard the bell ring by the gate and seen a man carrying a mound of lavender cellophane. He'd thought, at first, the guy was holding a wadded-up pool cover. The basket (he saw that it had a handle) had been brought in the side-car of a motorcycle. The man held it, wordlessly, until he came close enough to receive it. Tied below the bow was a large card the man gestured to, decorated with a computer-generated palm tree and a half moon.

EVERYTHING HERE IS MEANT TO SUSTAIN

THESE ARE SOME GOODIES TO LESSEN THE PAIN

SOON THE TROPICS WILL FLOURISH AND ORCHIDS WILL BLOOM

AND WE'LL ALL GO ABOUT WITHOUT SUCH DARK GLOOM

FOR THE PLANET IS OLD AND IT HAS SEEN WORSE

THAN HURRICANE WILMA WHO GAVE US HER CURSE.

SINCERE WISHES FOR A BETTER TOMORROW,
JUDY

Through the cellophane, he could see a bottle of champagne and the familiar printing on a box of Carr's Water Crackers. The thing weighed a ton. He decided it was best to hold it with both hands. Though the outside wrapping was a mess, what was inside looked more orderly than the street in front of the house. Bruce squinted and made out a box of chocolate-covered macadamias.

"So I guess you've got a pretty nice friend. I came all the way from Marathon," the man said. "I guess your friend doesn't mind spending money. The delivery charge, I personally wouldn't have paid."

A blond girl sat on the back of the motorcycle, wearing red boots, shorts, and a halter top. She was tan. Earphones were clamped over her head. She never looked in their direction.

"I'm not—" he began.

"Not what? Not somebody who'd expected a poem I took down like I was a goddamned executive secretary with a plaid skirt and health insurance and life insurance and my free annual breast exam? No, I'm somebody who can provide a shitload of gourmet food. You're a hard-working American who'll take pleasure in whatever comes your way, right, buddy? Not everybody has to be working the soup kitchen, right? I'm not, myself."

"I'm just visiting. Listen, man, thanks a lot."

The man had a broad chest and long sideburns. He cocked his head. He expected a tip? On top of what he, himself, all but said was exorbitant payment?

"Some girl got a crush on you?" the man asked, raising his eyebrows again and flipping the card with his thumb. Something moved around in his cheek, maybe gum.

"Nobody I know. I'll just be taking this in for the owners."

"Owners of a nice Victorian. You wouldn't be that owner, would you? Restored very nice. Property taxes you can afford, or you wouldn't be standing here."

"It's not my house," he said.

"Not your dog, either?"

Folly had come to stand at his side, tail slowly wagging. He and the dog had had tuna fish for lunch. He'd found three cans and given the dog two of them. The dog sniffed the man's fingers.

Bruce raised his hands, palms up. The gesture was spontaneous, but had bad results: it made him feel bereft, alone, and helpless. "I'm twenty-one," he said. "You think people my age have houses like this?"

"Trust-fund kids do," the man said. He flexed his fingers. Folly stepped back.

"Lost a lot of stuff in the hurricane," the man said. "Some woman calls from Maine, probably the same day she's scheduling her annual *breast exam,* wants me to take down her poem—don't mind if it's a long one—*exactly.* 'Read it back, read it back.' Bitch wants me down here *today.*"

"Henry!" the girl in the earphones said. Could she hear them, or was she just tired of waiting? She planted her hands on her knees and stared straight ahead.

"Since it's not yours," the man said, leaning in a bit, "don't guess you'd mind opening it and giving me one of those cheese balls and a box of crackers?"

"Listen, I'm sorry you lost stuff. I guess I should be going inside," he said. The dog waited, looking nowhere in particular. The basket was heavy, but he felt like a sissy for holding the handle with both hands. He said, "I was with a girl who locked herself up during the storm, didn't speak to me all day and night, like it was my fault or something, then just walked out. Not even a goodbye." The dog furled its brow. Then it resumed its mid-distance stare. "You want cheese, is that it?" he said, lowering the basket to the sidewalk.

"I mean it!" the blonde hollered.

"Ball buster," the man said, under his breath. He tapped the toe of his boot against the basket. He said: "You enjoy your treats from your sweetheart, trust-fund boy." He turned and walked toward the motorcycle. A tattoo of something with a long, curled tail was on the back of one bicep. The blonde flipped her hair over her shoulder. As they drove off, he was surprised to see her flip him the finger. He wanted his old life back, that was all he wanted. He picked up the basket, which crinkled noisily in his hands. It sounded the way the hurricane had sounded: tinny and way too loud. He thought the girl might have been mad at him because he got distracted by the storm so soon after sex. But they were in a hurricane, for god's sake! Didn't she realize he'd been upset? His heart was pounding now. He went through the gate, looked back for Folly, who had placed a paw on a banana peel. All around it were coffee grounds, like a broken scab. The dog nosed a mangled hibiscus, then hung his head and walked through the gate.

He flipped the lock hard. Stupid dog, he found himself thinking. Stupid people, to own this place in the tropics, a four-mile-long hurricane magnet. They were obviously people oblivious to living with anxiety. They were, in fact, just what the motorcycle guy knew them to be: rich and numbed by wealth. They were fortunate—knowing people who sent them presents. If the basket were his, he'd donate it to the homeless, or to the people who no longer had refrigerators and stoves. Large tented areas had been quickly erected—one right around the corner on Simonton—to feed people hot meals after the hurricane. He'd even seen a rooster heading in that direction. He put the basket on the kitchen counter, wondering, vaguely, whether anything inside would spoil if it wasn't refrigerated. He hated champagne but felt like opening it, shaking the bottle first, really making the cork fly.

"Do it again!" the girl had squealed on the granite counter, her dry heels like brush bristles against his sides, her breath a breeze of minty toothpaste with undertones of Johnnie Walker. Then for no reason she'd locked herself in the bathroom and never spoken to him again.

He saw them coming toward the house: the bags, the rolling suitcase. He jumped up. He should go down to meet them. Their welcome basket awaited, their dog was fine. They'd embrace Folly and pretend they were relieved that *he* was also fine. He'd pretend to be. What was he going to do, take Paul aside and ask for a little information, man-to-man? Or maybe he *was* okay: not as lucky as a trust-fund kid, but still lucky. Who wanted a nutcase for a girlfriend? The car his parents had given him had no damage. He'd ridden out the hurricane (wasn't that the expression? He'd ridden the girl, she'd ridden him, a real couple of buckaroos they'd been, and then something had happened and she had gone into the bathroom and locked the door). He could hit the road now, get off this ruined island.

Casey was smiling wanly at him. Paul had him fixed with his eye. Tired travelers who didn't know anything: they'd stay in the dark about the goings-on inside the house, be so grateful to him for taking care of their precious pooch. They'd be delighted with their gift basket of food. (The dog had begun to descend the stairs.) How long would it take for them to figure out the scotch had been diluted? Or would they care? What, exactly, would seem like the end of the world to people like Casey and Paul? (The dog, in the stairwell, had been stopped by the closed door at the bottom. Bruce opened the door.) Once the debris had been cleaned out by the pool service and the pool refilled, Paul would be painting the moon's wavering reflection again, Casey was saying a bit hysterically, crouching to scramble her fingers through the dog's ruff, and she'd be upstairs. She'd be the lady who exclaimed, who unwrapped presents as if she deserved them, as if being lucky was all a matter of keeping in motion, and she was as fleet as the wind.

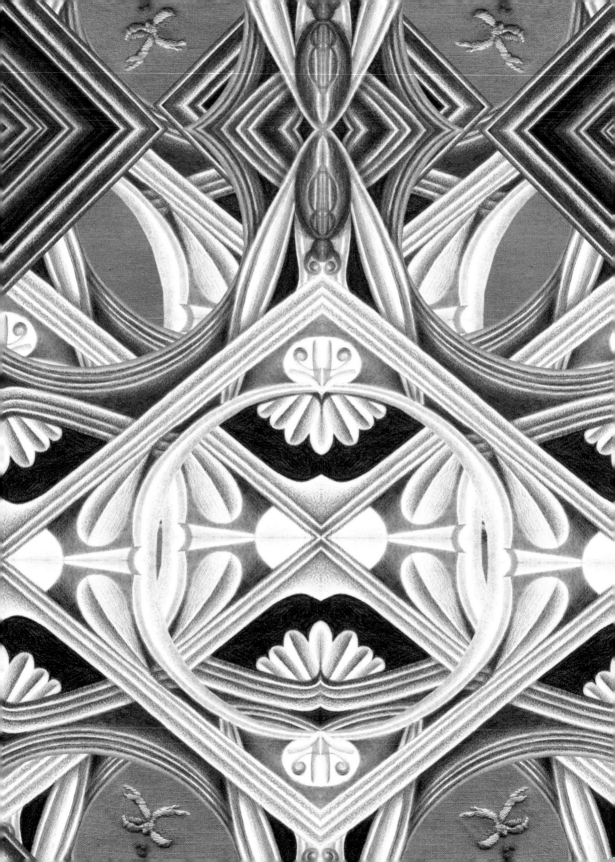

Chris Bachelder

My Son,
There Exists
Another World
Alongside Our Own

DEAR SON,

Your mother reports, nigh hysterically, the locked doors, crusty socks, slow-moving drains. To hear her tell it, the old Tudor may be washed Biblically away by your emissions. She needs, as always, to simmer down. You are not troubled and this is not troubling news. Nor is it news at all: When you were here last month I came upon your sad, dappled portfolio of beaver, torn from magazines and faded as if from the intensity of your gaze. It cannot be long now, if I correctly recall the order of things, before you are down on the hairy bathmat, conspiring to play your own flute. It is a job best outsourced, my boy; though rare and wondrous, auto-fellation is, erotically and spiritually speaking, a cul-de-sac.

More to the point, your mother reckons that it is time I, parenting-wise, "clock in." "For once," she adds. I presume that Jim, lacking not only testes but also vertebrae and a cerebral cortex, is not up for the task. Thus it falls to me, your biannual custodian, to impart certain vital facts. Rest assured, this is not about mechanics. No doubt you have some understanding of the hot spots and ancient maneuvers. They say a fetus in utero will suck its thumb if its thumb floats into its mouth, and I trust that you too would instinctually know how and what to suck should you find it moving slowly faceward.

Son: One of the mysteries of putative adulthood is why, when we have the wherewithal to bring our genitals into almost constant contact with another's, we do not. You are shy and weird, as I was. My guess is that you find yourself perpetually alienated from the cooch. But you will hear stories—some sophomore no doubt allowed (invited, some say) a wrestler to invade her with a candy cane. In May, no less. A bearded ninth-grader in a neighboring district screwed an earth-science teacher in a musty supplies closet, her dress, one imagines, shoved up around her pale hips. Her mug shot in the local *Messenger* is nothing much, but still.

You will begin to suspect that there exists a parallel universe—precisely identical to ours but for the fact that its inhabitants engage in frequent, vigorous, and thrillingly filthy congress, bounded only by the human imagination, a dwindling list of taboos, and certain very real physical limitations. You will suspect sex on public transport, sex beneath restaurant table, sex behind yonder rock. Son, if my letter has a single point, it is this: In such suspicion *you will be right.* This world—oh how I wish someone had told me this as I am telling you now—this parallel world is real and it is richly inhabited. Furthermore, and this is important, even a pigeon-toed asthmatic will, based on little else than dumb luck or the blind laws of probability, espy the world's entrance.

It is closed to me now, my boy. I am forty-six years old. I was married to your mother for fourteen years. And while I fondly recall slurping Budweiser from her lovely belly button in a Sarasota hotel room, mid-afternoon, this sort of frolicsome spirit was, ultimately, unsustainable. Before your mother, the girls I dated were meek and misinformed. One of them, having heard that sperm *swim* toward the female gamete, was convinced that they could swim great distances—i.e., across bedsheets and car seats, up stairs or pant legs. After her punishing hand jobs—pretty much the pinnacle of our erotic career—she would hightail it from the room, fleeing my puddling spunk. And at present there is Melinda, whom you will remember from your last visit. Melinda, whom I met on eDestiny with my fraudulent e-bio. Melinda is a real sweetheart, no doubt about it, and a wonderful companion. She enjoys cooking meals together and she absolutely loves animals. She does not, however, carry a tiger-striped dildo in her tote bag. The list of things I've never done, that have never been done to me, will not taper in the Era of Melinda. So be it.

As a conscripted but zealous pedagogue, though, I feel compelled to tell you that your father has thrice beheld the portal to this universe and has thrice refused to enter. It is my hope that this confession can at least enrich the life of my sole descendant.

When I was twenty-three, well beyond my sexual prime but still pretty jumpy, I worked as a caterer in Houston. The theme of one memorable catering event required the swaying and feather waving of two authentic Brazilian dancers, lovely and coked, with glittery thongs. While serving smoked-trout tostados, I stole glances at these bored beauties, felt the thickening in my flame-retardant pants. When, at the end of the evening, I was instructed to carry a large bouquet out of the hall for the dancers, I followed them to a bathroom, where I presumed they would change out of their glittery thongs and into something more sensible. I drew up outside, uncomfortably, politely. The first dancer disappeared into the bathroom, but the second one turned in the doorway, giggled, and beckoned me with her finger, saying, "Eet's okay. Eet's okay." This, son, was a wormhole. I ask you now as I have asked myself for nearly twenty-five years: Might this not have been an interesting moment in an otherwise undistinguished life? Might middle age have descended less violently had I spent eight to twelve squalid minutes in a bathroom stall with at least one and as many as two subequatorial dancers? I admit that up close the beckoner looked quite young, tired, and bereft of that ocular twinkle that we call the soul or life force, but it was fear, not pity, that froze me behind the enormous bouquet. Among my fears: Women, Brazil, feathers, glitter, bathrooms, VD, paternity, the hairless mons. Standing at the mouth of the portal, my son, I put down the bouquet and I fled. Eet was not okay.

The second time I beheld the shimmering threshold was near the end of an office Halloween party at which I wore a long dress, makeup, and a wig. That night I drank a staggering amount of punch ladled from a pumpkin, and by party's end, I'll admit, I very much wanted someone to hike my skirts and have at me. The portal, it glimmered and pulsed: A she-monster from Human Resources, blood-spattered and married, asked me for a ride home "or anywhere else." She was tall and lean, frantic, with half a cigar tucked behind her ear. I declined—more accurately, I stared at her bloody cleavage and lapsed into a vegetative state. When I came to, she was leaving with Reed Munson (accounting), who was costumed as Reagan *and* Gorbachev. This was near the end of the Cold War, son. The next day

Munson told me she had lain perfectly still on the bed, divested of costume, and asked him, repeatedly, to "fuck her like a horse." Like a horse, son! As in: "Will you? Will you? Will you fuck me like a horse?" I concede the ambiguity—did she wish to be fucked as if *she* were the horse? As if *Munson* were the horse? Or simply in the *manner* of horses?—but my God, just to be asked that by a naughty HR gal with fake wounds. Munson went about it with full equine intent, but the next day he was sick and ashamed, dreading the workweek. He told me I was smart and lucky to have escaped, but that is not the way I saw it then, and it is not the way I see it now.

About the third time I will remain circumspect. Let me just say it involved a dude. A dude with an extraordinarily lurid and specific proposal. He was young and fit—even his face was muscular. My first thought, it's true, was of my incipient girth, the little pouches of flab at the confluence of arm and chest. I remember looking out at the gravel-studded banks of plowed snow beyond the window of the saloon where I had come to celebrate the birth of Christ. (You, I believe, were eating figgy pudding, decking the halls of Jim's raised ranch.) The homosexual elaborated his proposition, and I heard him out, staring at my hairy thumbs. I have never gone in for that kind of thing, son, but as I approach fifty I do wonder if you can claim to have lived a full and meaningful life without ever having had something stuck up your rear. It is with something close to regret that I recall my terse refusal, my hasty exit, my impetuous holiday drive, culminating—you may remember this—in Jim's front yard.

I mention only the three occasions I am sure of; at other times I am almost certain I have glimpsed the portal. The trained eye no doubt sees a world of doors and tunnels—just because that woman smiling at you on the Greyhound is six months pregnant, do not assume she does not have prurient designs. Do not assume, as I did, that her designs are somehow adverse or untoward. The portal is a gift, I have realized.

I have slept on this letter, as the watchdogs of civility instruct. Indeed, last night I seem to have drunk myself atop it! This morning I have reread it and I find it holds up nicely. I will be sending a duplicate to your mother and Jim as evidence of fulfilled paternal duties.

Son, if this letter has a single point, it is this: Go forth, rubbered and steeled. Go. When you see the portal—and you will see it—enter it, penetrate it. Eet's okay. Screw it with your very person. Seek asylum, citizenship on the other side. If there be sadness, loneliness, and regret Over There, well, honestly, could it possibly be any greater than what we know Here?

Clocking out,

Your father

H E CAME BACK AT LAST to make her his wife.

Or not exactly.

One thing that happened while Davids was away was that the woman he loved had met an office-supply-store manager, married him, bought a house in the west suburbs, and then had a difficult birth that resulted in a too-small baby who gradually grew to be not quite too small and then about normal-sized and whose presence Davids had, from afar, heard rumors of prior to the baby's separate existence from the woman he (formerly) loved and then heard of again officially by announcement from the happy family itself—a preprinted card inside an envelope with a bit of tissue, the entire inside an additional envelope.

So, as custom commands, he sent a gift in the name of friendship because that is what he supposed they were now—friends—and he put his belongings back into boxes and moved back, not to make her his wife.

Who was she now?

She phoned of all things.

Come see us, she said of all things. I'm having a party. Bring someone.

Come meet my husband, she said.

I think I'd rather not, he said.

I'd rather just see you, he said.

I'm a two now, she said. Actually a three. So if you want to see me, you see us all.

Where had he been all this time?

He had left (her) in the first place because she used to say with frequency and urgency that she might chuck everything at any moment, why she might run away to the city! Except she couldn't, she said, because she lived in a city and you can't run away to someplace if you're there. She said it so convincingly that he himself ran away—to a small town, if you please, took a temporary job transfer, with plans to come back when she asked, which she didn't. A year passed. He heard things. An office-supply-store manager. A wedding. The ice sculptures at the wedding. They had had melting ice and strewn petals and strolling troubadours. And he thought it unfair of her to go off and take care of things so neatly and quickly, in under two short years, while he'd been sitting in that small town waiting for her to want him. Then he came back to the city, not because his temporary transfer ended and he was sent back (it hadn't, he quit) but because he'd been away for nearly two long years—in which time marriage, house, child, etc.—and he hadn't found anything he wanted in that town and had found plenty he did not.

I sent you a gift, he said.

Oh yes, she said. We got it. We're months behind in our thank-yous. I'm sorry. We're getting to your thank-you.

(We.)

I don't need a thank-you.

I always send thank-yous.

You may toss my thank-you in the trash.

But I do want to thank you.

I feel thanked, I'm thanked. Thank you.

Thank *you*.

You're welcome.

* * *

Why did he have to sound like such a bully? Pushing her around, demanding or not demanding thank-yous?

In the end he agreed to go to the party and meet the office-supply-store manager and the actual child now in existence but still small. Agreed to go despite the fact that everything appeared to be wrong where he was living, dark all the time, more so than in other neighborhoods, and his new job was awful, not as bad as all that, but uncomfortable—unfamiliar people younger than him, less educated, watery coffee in the break room, a billboard for ovens outside his window, a slab of tile on the floor, the usual mayhem on the street, agreed to go despite the fact that while he was still on the phone, linking triangles on his scratch pad, she said something about the curtains, about choosing them, and what she said was: It's loads of fun.

He himself did not use those words to describe his experience, ever.

Then she said, Want to hear the baby coo? Listen.

He heard something, it might have been what she wanted.

Did you hear? Did you hear him coo? Now he's not doing it.

He drove out to the suburbs, followed the directions the woman he once loved had given him and he couldn't believe how far it was and how many highways got involved. It was a vast plain out there, everything beige or gray, rectangles and horizontals, tollbooths, flat fallow fields. Gasoline signs jutted into the sky. He kept driving. He drove until he thought he was lost and would have to stop on these cloned roads, turn back, return without what he'd come for (her) or with what he'd meant to drop off (present, wrapped square in trunk, containing elementary puzzle). He drove until he thought it might be a trick, that she'd sent him out here, or that someone else was playing the trick, on her, had tossed her here and left and she needed to be saved, not by him but by someone else, a leaf man, a snow blower, or, worse, she didn't need saving, somehow this itself was the salvation, or protection, from something she'd witnessed or done or was tempted to do. And then he saw, pulling up (because he wasn't lost after all), that it was not a joke, could not have been, that this was serious business because how else could she have ended up on this obstacle-course board amid all the hollow blocks, all the empty landscapes of one's dreams? Lines of houses, different from military issue only in the most superficial aspects. A mailbox that looked like a reindeer, a soggy doll fastened to a swing.

He sat in his car at the end of the block. He did not want to go through with this.

Then the woman he loved was coming out of the house, a regular-sized baby in her arms, held awkwardly, looking exactly the same as she always had, exactly, coming over the lighted grass to greet the other guests just arriving, hadn't seen him yet at the end of the block, sitting in the growing dark, low behind the wheel. Was it beautiful, that exact way she looked? Was it not beautiful? He couldn't tell, he knew her so well, had such physical pain when he looked at her, he couldn't tell what she looked like at all.

Witnesses: none. No one looked his way. Everyone looked at the bright figures on the lawn.

He pulled away, drove right by.

Another part of their conversation on the phone went like this:
I'm sorry about the way things turned out. I meant to tell you.
You did, he said. You did tell me. I got the card.
Card?
You sent me a card. An announcement.

He stopped to get a sandwich. Had to. He could not swallow this *and* the chunks of meat the office-supply-store manager would stab off the grill. The place he stopped was a bar near the entrance of the highway, just the sort of place he'd avoided all his life, built of chrome or plastic, a gleaming orange square, the entire structure, whatever it was, however they'd molded the thing down so it stood on its plot without tipping over like a tinker.

He went in.

There was a wedding party in there, in this sports place, and he sat down at the bar, ordered a tuna-snack which he would eat and then go back not to claim her.

The bride and one of the groomsmen came over and sat on one side of him, the bride beside him in her giant dress which she moved with her arms like carrying laundry. Look at those legs, Davids heard her say to the groomsman. She reached out and touched the groomsman's thigh.

Davids moved his food away from them and shifted on his stool.

I'd like to feel those around my waist one night, the bride said.

Davids waved for the check.

Then a man who had to be the groom came walking over in a slouch. What the hell is going on here, he said. One hour into the thing and you're flirting?

I'm not flirting, she said. I'm conversing.

Looks like you're flirting, he said. Oh lord and on our wedding night, he said. What have I done.

We were not flirting, said the groomsman.

I'd just believe that from you, said the groom.

Well, now, said the bride. There's an easy way to resolve this. Let's ask this objective observer for a factual opinion. I, she laid her hand across her heart, swear that I have never witnessed this man until these few minutes that have been passing. And with her other hand, the ringed one, she gestured to Davids, who had been sitting quietly, who was just getting up, leaving his tuna untouched, leaving a bill on the bar, was going to see loved woman, husband, child, house, curtains, and so forth.

Once, by the way, he himself had saved her. He wondered if she remembered, if she ever threw it in the manager's face when she felt wronged. Said his name and "saved my life." It happened on top of a mountain in Colorado. She had gotten heat stroke, had nearly died up there. He had gotten her down, not lost his head.

All right, said the groom, straightening. Let's have it then. Was she flirting with this man? They looked at Davids.

I don't know. Yes, I suppose, admitted Davids—because she was! Although later, after some review, he thought perhaps that moment might have been an opportunity to introduce a diversion, ask how the fine couple had met, etc., what they had whipped up for their honeymoon—Amsterdam? Guam?—that perhaps he might have let the poor groom be fooled for the first hours of his catastrophic marriage, let the poor bride enjoy her few days of pre-alimonious existence. This thought came to him because the poor groom at this moment looked as if he'd been struck and the other groomsmen came over and the bridesmaids came over.

You cheating whore! the groom said hoarsely, like a song.

The bridesmaids and the groomsmen—miraculously the flirting groomsman now among them—joined as one voice, stood as one body, and accused. You flirt!

He's lying! she said, but they knew better.

On your own wedding day no less, they said.

Then, in a move Davids didn't quite understand, couldn't follow the logic—they led the groom out sniffling and then they were gone. Left the bride frowning beside Davids, in her wedding dress, hand clasped around her shell of champagne. Davids couldn't believe it.

Now look what you've done, she said, turning on him. She was incredibly young and indeed he did feel a little ashamed of himself but she was the one who flirted, not him, and she should have behaved herself and he would tell her so.

You should have behaved yourself, he said.

Don't you start with me, she said. You of all people. Look, here I am alone on my own wedding night.

That's not my fault, he said. (He wasn't sure about that.)

Yes, it is and you're going to give me a ride home as soon as I finish this drink.

No, I'm not.

Yes, you are, unless you want me to go out and look for a rent-a-car and then use a credit card which I don't even have and then drive home under the influence of alcohol and get put in prison on my very wedding night.

And where are your parents on this evening when they certainly should be here with you? he said.

Not here!

I suggest that you phone them and tell them what you've done.

What, that I got married or that my husband left me?

He considered this. How far away do you live? he asked.

Close, she said. Two exits up the highway.

One time he had written the woman he (no longer) loved a letter. *I feel like I'm investing a lot in this,* he wrote. *I have to get something back from you to keep this going.* She may have been engaged by that time.

So he let her get in his car—now he had an actual bride with him with all of her petticoats or hoops or whatever she had under there filling up the front seat and he had to physically move her dress out of the way (which is almost like touching her which he did not want to do) so he could get to the shift. The night was beginning to feel eternal and this really was pathetic, this was bad. He drove out of the parking lot, she complaining the whole time. You just had to have your say-so, she said. Why couldn't you have kept your mouth shut? This, while he hollered over her, May I remind you, miss, that you solicited my opinion? Maybe next time you shouldn't ask if you don't want the truth known to the wider public. They went on like that until she shouted, Exit here, this exit here.

He pulled off the highway. Turn, she said. Turn. Here we are. Stop.

They sat, stopped and gasping.

This is no house, he said, because it wasn't. It looked like some sort of fallout shelter, nickel-plated and pulsing.

I can't go home yet, she said. I have to wait for him to calm down. You saw how upset he was. Let's go to the club and wait it out.

What? The what?

The club, it's a dance club. Let's go in, just for half an hour, then I'll go home. It's right here. She pointed.

You said we were going to your house.

A stop. A quick stop. One drink, then home.

This is not the party bus, he said.

I'm already late for my visit, he said.

No way, he said.

Look, this is your responsibility. I'm likely to wind up divorced because of you. Divorced after one day of marriage, who could be so unlucky as that? So you better take me wherever I want to go and I want to dance one dance on my wedding night and drink one drink as a happily married woman and then I want to go home to my husband who will then divorce me because of what you did which you never should have in the first place.

And then she said, You owe me, mister.

And then she said, You're an evil man.

He was hurt. I would like you to think about how unfair that is, he said.

What he could say: Lady, I have another wife to go see.

But he may as well play the whole record to the scratchy end. Well, I may as well, he said, as long as it doesn't take too long because I have to be somewhere and I am now running very, very (he looked at his watch), *very* late. Honest to God. Jesus, he said and pulled into the parking lot.

And you may keep your curses of the Lord's name to yourself because I do not want even to hear that just now, thank you, she said.

The club was worse than he could have imagined or just as bad at least. It was late enough now that people had begun dancing. He sat at the bar with a plain orange juice in front of him because he was not going to show up at the home of the woman he formerly loved smelling of liquor. The bride danced alone in her dress. Still, men started to dance with her. One by one they approached.

Everybody looked a little regretful out there, the bride stumbling a bit, one of them taking her elbow so she didn't topple over. Davids put down his orange juice, stood, headed for the outside—because who wouldn't take advantage of these few colored-light-studded moments to make his escape, who wouldn't? Was he supposed to remain stuck to this bride for what could turn out to be the rest of his life? He himself felt a little regretful, a little melancholy, and it was a sad solemn moment for them all. He paused at the door, turned back, saw her, white and streaming. He remembered another time he had left her. They were on a subway, coming home from dinner, and he had jumped out at the wrong stop, left her there alone on the train, angry over a slight. Or there was the time he had stormed out of her apartment. Or the other time he had stormed out of her apartment. Or another time in the car in the midst of an argument he had gotten out at a light. She didn't go when the light turned green, sat there while people honked.

Who could want a man like that?

Oh, fine, he said and stomped back. He took her by the wrist and dragged her out the door.

Now she was back in the car with him. Okay, you had your fun, he said, pulling out of the parking lot. And now you're going home. Where do you live? Hello? Where do you live?

And she wasn't answering because she was asleep.

Terrific, this is just what I need, he said. Hey, he said, hey. Can you hear me?

She was completely passed out. Hey, he said. Wake up. He kept driving. Is this your house? he said. Is it this one? Or this one? Just tell me that much. I'll do the rest. He stopped at a stop sign. The street was deserted. He stared out the windshield. The pavement shone like a river, houses were strung along their plots of lawn. He had no idea where he was. Squares and squares and squares of blocks multiplied away from their little car. The bride slept. He called to her again but he did not know her name.

He got back on the highway but it was really late now. Her street was dark, the lawn unlit, though the small diamond lamp by the door still burned. Oversight? Expectation? He knocked on the door and waited. The woman he loved, robed and yawning, opened the door. It's rather late, she said.

I was engaged, he said.

Everyone's gone.

I'm sorry.

(Pause.)

I'm glad you came by, she said stiffly, although he could see very well she was more glad he had left in the first place, what with this house and now this husband and baby coming up behind her saying Who is it? The thin stick of an office-supply-store manager who then shifted the lump of baby and sidestepped in front of her. He stuck out his hand. Any friend of my wife's, he said and stopped.

I brought a present, said Davids. It's in the trunk.

Bring it here, why not? she said.

He glanced back into the dark. I better not, he said.

They all stood, saying nothing.

I need to put the baby down, said the office-supply-store manager after a while.

And suddenly it seemed as though the whole ordeal was over, though it had hardly begun. Nobody was inviting or getting invited in. Everybody was exchanging a second solid handshake and getting a single light peck on the cheek and everyone seemed equally choiceless and drab, the destined meeting passing and fading. Then the woman he once loved stood alone in the doorway, the store manager gone off to put the baby away, her light-pink robe around her.

Let me get you out of here, he said.

Excuse me?

Come on, let's run away. We'll leave a note on the table: Gone dancing. I mean, what would you really miss? he said.

I mean, he said, what the hell is going on here? It looks like some kind of game out here, like some kind of maze—

My own life, he wept, leaning on the doorframe, is an affliction. My own home… he said, taking her hand. I know I can be a difficult man.

No, he didn't take her hand. No, he didn't say all that or he didn't think he did, not all of it. But he must have because the woman he loved, loves, was saying, Good Lord!, so he must have said some of it, but then again she wasn't looking at him as she said it, but behind him, over his shoulder. What is *that?* she said, withdrawing her hand (so he must have done that much—taken it). He couldn't bear to look but he did.

It was the bride, coming over the grass toward him, her dress trailing. Her face rubbed and pale. And he saw suddenly that she could be the answer. He could devote himself to helping her, to getting her off the drink, back in school. He would change her. He could make her, keep her cubbyholed if he had to, just let her try to get away. And after a few years she would fall in love with him—things like that do happen, you know. They would get married and move out to the suburbs, right next door to this very house. And they would have their own babies and name them the same names as *their* babies and he would take pictures at Christmas of his lovely wife and tots and put them in the mailbox of the woman he (once) loved who in this dream had shrunk down and was shuffling in a corner in a room.

But even as he stood between them he already knew his wife would disappoint him. She wouldn't go along with it, or wouldn't think the same way, or *be* the same way, or in some other way it would all be imperfect and flawed and defective. He could see it. It would always be like this—he'd be in the wrong house, living the wrong life, hefting ludicrous presents across wastelands and deserts, and in his rage at his marred fate, at her unscarred exit, he turned, lifted his arm, to do what? To embrace, to strike?

This, he said, is my bride.

HALF-MOON TERROR and I were talking politics at the edge of the swamp when the billionaire's son first appeared.

It was late afternoon, the sun spiking through a wall of brush on the far side of the lagoon, and just as Half-Moon pointed to a pair of alligator backs unzipping the skin of the water—"What does the Local Council plan to do with *those* guys, right? Can you tell a water monster, 'Be *Catholic*'? 'Don't be a man-eater: drop your dignity and your instinct and speak *Indonesian*'?"—just as he said this the forest began trembling with sound and the boat careered around a bulge of trees.

"Case in point," I said, meaning the boat. "Ready to receive the Eucharist, change your name?"

Half-Moon grunted. He hardly ever wore paint anymore, but as he squinted at the noise I thought I caught the former warrior in him twitching with hunger for a good invasion. Then he sighed.

"Those aren't priests," he said. "It's Bringing Man."

The boat slowed. It was a big white catamaran with greenish windows and battered twin hulls. Touching shore, it coughed and gargled and went quiet. Things had gotten so that the hullabaloo of a motored catamaran posed little threat to an Asmat. Traders, missionaries, art scholars—they all got here by boat. What made this weird for Half-Moon and me was seeing Bringing Man take such motherly care in getting a white visitor to shore.

Tossing a rope ladder over the side, Bringing Man climbed halfway down and then dropped thigh-deep into the water. The billionaire's son swung a thin leg over the railing. Bringing Man stood waiting to help him, one hand slightly higher than the other, his face a grimace of expectation. As he made reassuring sounds in a white language, the visitor's foot slipped. His body fell hard into the side of the boat, and he clung to the ladder desperately, his feet kicking the air while quick waves smacked our feet and lapped at the crotch of Bringing Man's military fatigues. Bringing Man cooed, and the visitor craned his neck to see the water below him. After a moment's hesitation, he flung himself away from the ladder and splashed into the swamp. They slogged to ground holding hands, grinning like bedmates.

"Mind if we pop in for a bit?" Bringing Man said.

"Is this one Dutch?" Half-Moon Terror demanded. "Because if he is—"

"Not Dutch," Bringing Man said. "Not even European!"

Next to him the visitor beamed, breathing hard. He had slender arms, a pale forehead glossed with sweat, and childish pink lips showing in an unsuccessful see-through beard. Absently he gripped the handle of the large knife in his belt and looked around in wonder. The lenses of his eyewear flashed in the late sun as he took it all in: the darkening green swamp, the high forest jingling with bird sounds, the mud-smelling air, a stick hut near the water where some wallaby hides lay tanning, Half-Moon and I naked except for the ornaments in our faces. Some hunters in the village had recently brought down a black pig, and from its pelvis I'd carved and imbued with magic a crescent to wear through my nose. This sharp-tipped moon was meant to bring fertility to my wife and me, and the billionaire's son stared at it without shame. Bringing Man clasped his shoulder and shook a quick laugh from him.

"This is Rockefeller," he said. "He's from a kingdom in America called New York, where his father is a major, *major* dignitary. In New York, remember, they have paper charms called *dollars,* and the Rockefeller tribe, well—they have quite a lot of these."

"What, like an armload?" Half-Moon said. "Or like a pile on the floor, or what."

"More like sands of a riverbed. That's what *billion* means, you savage. And to have this many paper charms makes one not only a king of sorts but also a *billion-aire.* Anyhow, there's a doctor with him, and a couple of helpers still on board—"

"BILL-yon," said Half-Moon Terror. He'd been fiddling with the barb of ivory in his bottom lip, and he quit doing this to tug philosophically at his foreskin.

"Bill-yon-ERR," I said, and slapped the white man in the chest. Half-Moon and I had seen paper before; we both despised its uselessness, and Rockefeller's love for it made him, among other things, a fool. Also that he would own a billion of anything, let alone *papers,* was a lunacy of surplus. One of the first things visitors learn here is that in Irian Jaya nobody owns more than the eye can absorb in a glance. "Take him back," I said.

"Hang on, now," Bringing Man said. "He's all the way from a palace of learning in his father's kingdom—*Har*-vard—where they're dying to show off your work."

"Bringing Man, I know what an archeologist is," I said.

"Right, I know, but listen. He tells me, before we left Java, he goes: 'Take me to Papua New Guinea, because I want desperately to find the master carver who made *this.*'"

Bringing Man made a sort of hurrying gesture to Rockefeller, who, fumbling with his shirt pocket, took out a fold of paper. He handed it to me. Bringing Man grinned like a thief.

"He's totally monkey shit over your stuff. And so I tell him: 'Good man, I'll show you not just where to look, I'll take you to *the guy*—Designing Man himself.'"

I unfolded the paper and saw a colorless image, bisected by a lightning-white crease: a clean-shaven Rockefeller, holding an Asmat neck rest patterned with cuscus tails and flying-fox feet, the heads of my father and grandfather carved into each end. I'd crafted it three or four seasons ago but couldn't remember what missionary I'd given it to or if I'd traded it for tobacco. In the picture Rockefeller wore a look of agreeable surprise, as though he'd been snuck up on and greeted warmly by an ancestor.

"You recognize it, right?" Bringing Man said. "You do, I can tell."

I gave Rockefeller back his picture.

"He's also got one of your ancestor poles, same design, and a shield. He's opening a museum in his kingdom. Says he'll pay anything."

I should point out here that Bringing Man was a Yali from the Central Highlands. All Yalis know in their hearts that money is the most worthless of all tradeable things; its primary magic needs at least two people to bring it out, always in a tingling moment of exchange. By oneself, in a dark immutable forest, it will lay forever inert like a broken spear or severed hand. Bringing Man knew all this, but he'd grown up working with his father repairing telephones on the main island, where he learned not only that trade but also a handful of white languages and some white geography and the hex of white dollars on men without talent, who, he discovered, made up much of the outer world. He earned a living by showing them the unshown, tooling them around the Irian Jayan coast on his boss's catamaran, and therefore couldn't help his spirit's bending over in money's presence.

"Bringing Man, what if I told you I was on semipermanent sabbatical?"

"I'd say *semipermanent* is an expensive word for *temporary*. I'd say that you, Designing Man, are the poorest fucker in your village, and that your wife would appreciate a little extra sago, as you guys are—no disrespect—semipermanently childless."

This stung. I must have made a face; Rockefeller looked hard at me, then to Bringing Man, who smiled fabulously and placed an assuaging hand on Rockefeller's chest. The two of them whispered a while, and it was during this pause that Half-Moon leaned close and kidded that we should take the billionaire's head.

In truth there hadn't been a beheading feast for who knew how long. We'd been a Dutch colony for ages, although lately Amsterdam had argued that we deserved to be a sovereign nation, complete with a striped flag and multilingual representatives in Jayapura. The Indonesians were about to adopt us as their own, believing we were the feral ancestry of their culture. What the Indonesians failed to acknowledge was that we Asmats, not to mention the Bauzi farther inland, the Korowai, Dani, Kamoro—even the Yalis like Bringing Man—weren't Indoanything. We were all the children of Melanesians from the South Seas, or so Bringing Man kept telling us. But it didn't matter. Already tribes at the edge of the mountains were dressing in pants like missionaries; their children were reading from brightly colored books and singing the French alphabet. The skull of an immortal's son could offer a cosmic boost in warding off more irreversible change. It was an edge against fate, and Half-Moon adored such edges. I was considering all of this when Rockefeller spoke up.

"Designing Man," he burst out in my language, "it would be my greatest elbow to stay for dinner."

"You mean *honor*," I said. It was clear he'd asked Bringing Man for the phrase. I shook my head. "Not *elbow*."

"You mean *honor!*" Rockefeller repeated.

"Elbow," Half-Moon Terror said, and grinned knowingly at me.

Our village sits in a clearing just deep enough in the forest that we can't see the water. We have eighteen huts in all, every one made of grass and sticks and vine and raised on stilts. They're identically cylindrical, with pointed, round roofs, except for the long feasting hall where we took Michael Rockefeller and his retinue. By the time Bringing Man, Half-Moon, and I had unloaded their gear, the air was darkening. My neighbors had gotten a fire roaring in the center of the village.

It was a decent blaze, with all manner of edible bugs swirling above the flames. The trees encasing the village towered black against a dark blue shell, my brownish hut flickering orange, a shadow man walking spastically under my feet, all this rippling color beating back the night and lifting me in a way that felt like the moment just prior to a discovery. My spirit was bursting in my chest. I rushed into the darkness of my hut to grab my headdress and sensed right away a breathing presence in the room.

Mad spirits are like this. They hover in the heads of trees and hang low over the dark water of the swamp, unable to reconcile the fact of their death with their own unspent energy. Occasionally an angry one slips unseen into the village. It is this sort of spirit, restless and bitterly afraid of being forgotten, that will shatter your glass trinkets from missionaries, smear feces on your oldest ancestor poles, or pounce crushingly on your chest while you dream. I could barely make this one out in the gloom, though by the chaos of feathers on top of it I could tell it had stolen my headdress.

"Go away, fucker," I said.

The shade jerked, and I heard my headgear hit the ground. A bad thing, as the centerpiece of its design happened to be the skull of my father. I let out a yell.

"Sorry!" My wife's voice. "Sorry, sorry, sorry."

"What—what are you doing?"

She was quiet for a long time. "Talking to your father."

"Ah," I said. "And what'd he say?"

"He said first of all don't be mad at me for putting on your things."

"I'm not mad, Breezy."

"He said you are. About a lot of stuff, only, you don't know it. He says you could be a little nicer."

"Can we pick this up later?" I said. "There's this white guy shown up from I forget the name of the place and Half-Moon's waiting for me down at the lodge, trying to get a feast going."

She stepped into the light, wearing a grass skirt and nothing else. "Can I come?"

"It's not that kind of feast."

I gathered up my headdress and a dogtooth necklace I planned to give Rockefeller and left her standing in the dark.

My wife's full name is Long Breeze Rousing The Forest In Hottest Summer And Swooshing Down To Gladden Our Hearts. Her father gave me a tame black pig for marrying her, but I would have done it for nothing. In my opinion she's the most inspired basket maker we have apart from Half-Moon's mother, and without a doubt she's the best cook. Her face is capable of the subtlest emotions, as well as a bounty of wry glances and reassuring smiles. We've been married eight seasons, but in this time the spirit world hasn't once seen fit to restore balance in our village by sending her a child, and people are starting to talk.

Every Asmat knows that the failure to receive offspring reflects a certain spiritual flaw in a woman, a displeasure among her ancestors, but to know Breezy is to understand how absurd this is. She's far too gentle and wise to rouse anger in this world, let alone in the realm of past fathers, and it's in her nature to use only good magic, and this strictly in the service of others. If women were permitted at a visitor's first feast, she would've enchanted Rockefeller. As I hurried to join him I had to remind myself that the dead, who see everything at once, know best when to gift the living with parenthood.

When I entered the feasting house the Governor had already installed himself next to Rockefeller, his doctor, and Bringing Man. Half-Moon Terror was busy working the fire pit in the center of the room. The Governor had illuminated the contours of his face with swirls of starlike white dots, and his eyes were rimmed in red. His headgear contained an imperial riot of wild plumage. He beckoned with a look for me to come join him, and by this I knew Rockefeller had been grilling him about how business might be carried out, how much tobacco and rice and sago root it might take to get me to carve a load of treasure for him. I took a seat between Rockefeller and Bringing Man.

"He wants carvings," the Governor said right away. "As many as you can produce in three months, and you get to name the price."

I looked at Rockefeller, who smiled back at me. His thick eyewear showed a pair of fires in refracted miniature. I took out my dogtooth necklace and drew it over his head.

"Let's work it out after dinner," I said.

All night Rockefeller waited to see what we would do and then mimicked our actions like a little boy. We had skewers of plump sago worms, and when I held one over the fire, so did Rockefeller. Usually visitors tend to hesitate before biting the head off a grub, but Rockefeller threw himself recklessly into eating. He chewed carefully, with his eyes closed, devoting the whole of his spirit to the labor of tasting. There was fire-baked fish and roasted flying fox and partridge stuffed with sweet rice, and with each new flavor Michael Rockefeller slapped his knee and exclaimed something in outrageous delight. Half-Moon distributed sago cakes, which contained bits of fish and dried plum, and Rockefeller anxiously watched me break off a bite and hand it to him. When he popped the morsel into his mouth, his face seemed to bloom. He looked at me, nodding gravely, and seeing that tears had come to his eyes I couldn't help laughing. Rockefeller leaned into Bringing Man for a phrase to express his heart in my language. He turned to me and clasped my hand.

"I am a *monkey fucker,*" he said.

Bringing Man's face was struggling. He glanced at Half-Moon Terror, who sat grinning and chewing.

Rockefeller took the bone-handled knife from his belt and tried giving it to me. "Monkey fucker? I," he tapped his chest, "*monkey fucker—*"

Bringing Man snickered.

"That's not funny," I said.

"Yes it is," he said.

"Monkey fucker!" Rockefeller blurted.

"What was it he wanted to say?" I said.

"Just, you know, this was the greatest meal of his life, he wants to be brothers and so on. Look at him, though. He looks like the monkey type."

Next to him Half-Moon sat glaring at me. He cut eyes at Rockefeller, and with dreamlike slowness dragged an index finger across his throat.

Rockefeller stayed four days, gorging himself nightly at four feasts, and left with a promise to return in three months, as we'd agreed. I vowed to give him the finest work of my life—ancestor poles, war shields, all manner of noble figures in whatever colored woods I could find. Then, two days after Rockefeller's boat pulled away to roam the coastline, our Governor was found dead in his hut.

There was no wound. It was as though he'd fallen down and his spirit had leapt out of him. The underchiefs were furious—he'd talked at length with Rockefeller's doctor at the first feast, and a few of them speculated that this man had somehow hexed the Governor, or poisoned him. In any event, they insisted, our tribe and Rockefeller's were now out of balance.

Years ago, before we were polluted by certain imported virtues, such an imbalance would have meant that someone of power in the rival tribe would have to part with his head. On our walks together, Half-Moon wouldn't leave it alone.

"This means Rockefeller," he said at the edge of the swamp. "But you're the one who's got the deal going with him."

"What are you getting at? I'm supposed to say either way?"

"Designing Man, our Governor's dead. We're leaderless. Until a new one's appointed the entire council has to agree how we handle this—and you, Master Carver, are a key player in this council."

"You sound like fucking Bringing Man right now, you know that."

"I'm just saying."

"Look, however the Governor died, that man, Rockefeller, is no enemy. You can't prove it's Rockefeller's fault. Next to my own wife he might be the least injurious soul I've met."

Half-Moon laughed. "What, because he's a fan of your work? Because he likes to *eat?*"

He had a point. I couldn't have said for sure what it was about Rockefeller that made me want to protect him, other than maybe his earnestness at the feast and his naive thirst for my brotherhood. But when I tried to imagine taking his head I could only see stars pouring out of his neck and a flock of enraged spirits descending on me in a scream.

"I'm voting no," I said.

Half-Moon behaved coolly toward me for the rest of the day. On my way back to the swamp for new wood, I spotted him at the edge of the village, holding court with two councilmen. They wanted an argument, it looked like—they were speaking harshly and gesturing toward my hut, and I was moved to see Half-Moon working to calm them. Something inside me, an oppressive tautness I hadn't noticed, untwisted and went slack.

Early the next morning I was jolted awake by Half's warrior voice roaring my full name.

Breezy lay sprawled beside me, sleep purring from her nostrils. I hadn't yet consulted her about the Rockefeller situation; the Asmat wife can be an unrelenting persuader in matters of beheading, man-eating, and magic, good or bad. For all her gentleness, I couldn't shake the worry that she'd disagree with me and then never let up. She sprang awake just as the first cry came from outside.

"Mother?" she said. She looked wildly around the room. Then, comprehending where she was, she rubbed her eyes. "I had the most horrible dream, about—is that somebody calling you?"

I got to my feet and walked naked to the door. In the center of a ring of onlookers stood Half-Moon Terror, painted in the style of his warrior days: his right side entirely black, his left, moon-white. He had an ancestor shield—one of my creations—on one arm. Next to him stood his wife, her belly gigantic with Half-Moon's forthcoming child, her breasts painted red and white like the eyes of an angry cockatoo.

"Great Designer And Carver Of Judicious Trees Into Forms Appearing Spirited Enough As To Respire And Know Our Fathers?" he repeated in a ceremonial tone. "With highest respect and goodwill I formally offer you, my brother, an exchange."

Half-Moon knew he had me here. Our brotherhood ritual had taken place long before I'd married Breezy, before I'd become master carver. When we were skinny young men we'd devoured the back meat of the Korowai warrior who beheaded his father. We'd shared our bodies in pleasurable ways, vowed to sacrifice our lives to spare the other. For me to refuse trading him Breezy for his wife Plentiful would not only undo this brotherhood but also be considered a grave social infraction.

"Oh for fuck's sake, Half."

"Brother," he went on, "I hereby give you my Plentiful Bliss, Plentiful Season, for whatever you would give to me in return."

I went back inside to discuss it with Breezy. She was already striping her torso in red, white, and black.

"Tell him to hang on," she said. "I'll be right out."

I stood there not saying anything. Breezy wrapped her waist in a new grass skirt.

"Have you seen my fox-fur headpiece? The red one?"

"Wait, stop," I said. "What about the pig? We could give him our pig?"

"A pig's a pig, Designing," she said. "Not a wife."

She remembered then that she'd loaned the headpiece to her sister. Taking up her old brown one, made of dog fur and tiny white shells, she walked past me without a word. I stepped outside, wanting to stop her, to murder my grinning brother, and saw Plentiful Bliss crossing the dirt to greet me.

"This is such an honor," she said. Plentiful had an enormous top row of square teeth, so her lips never quite touched. Her ears were small. The whites of her eyes were almost lost to her fat black irises, and her skin, I realized at that moment, was the exact reddish brown of the flying-fox headpiece my Breezy had been looking for. "Designing Man, wow."

"Let us all rejoice in this exchange," Half-Moon said to the whole village. "This pact between families."

Everyone, the councilmen and their wives, the weavers and hunters and bedecked warriors, raised their voices in celebration. I stayed quiet, staring at Breezy. She was smiling meekly, with downcast eyes.

"Okay then," Half-Moon said. "Back to what you were doing."

Soon as the crowd began to break, Plentiful reached between my legs and took hold of my shaping tool.

"Want to lie down?" she said.

Half-Moon raised his shield to me in salute. He turned to go back to his hut, and Breezy followed him.

"I guess so," I said.

There is no word in the Asmat language for what the missionaries call "love." We've always had some inkling of the concept, though, even without a term to solidify it in thought, and this, I believe, has left the feeling as unspoiled as the Asmat people used to be, before the Dutch conquered us and the missionaries came and the Main Island decided to make us Indonesian. In the week following Half-Moon's exchange ceremony I found myself awake nights turning this word over in my mind, tasting it, or trying to, the way Rockefeller had explored the manifold textures of a roasted sago worm. And yet each time I felt close to discovery, just shy of the riches in that basket of a word, Plentiful would roll over.

"The baby's still a little lumpy," she'd whisper. "I can feel it. Do you mind, just..."

And then shaping again. The lopsidedness of Half-Moon's child proved to be the foundation of my new marriage. In her quest for excellence, Plentiful awoke with relentless cravings which, no matter how often we shaped through daylight, harried her well into dark. But it wasn't until the third or fourth night that she had the nerve to bring up Rockefeller.

"I've been meaning to ask if you've given much thought to that recent visitor—what was his name?"

She was reclining on her right side, one leg suspended by a hand gripping her thigh. I was shaping Half's baby from this angle with hard, driving strokes, which took some pretending on my part.

"You want to talk about that now?"

"Well, it's just that things are *so* out of balance." Her voice quavered with the violence of my pelvis. "Don't you think?"

"I'm not thinking at the moment."

"Yeah, but, I mean we don't even have a Governor. Probably won't get one until—did Half mention this to you already?"

"Many times. Pick your leg up a little, please."

"I think it's a good idea. You know what I'm talking about?"

I stopped, breathless. "That's enough shaping for tonight."

"But what about the feeding? You can't stop before, you know, *nourishing* the baby, can you?"

"Yes, I can."

There were, all told, thirteen more nights of this, each with an increasingly detailed assessment of the Rockefeller situation: the spiritual imbalance between tribes, the daily rotting of my character in the eyes of the village council, how my drinking of a billionaire's spirit could make *me* Governor, possibly even a better carver. During the day I couldn't focus on the work I'd promised Rockefeller. Then one night she changed her tactic.

"You have to be worried," she said, on her back, knees raised. "Sooner or later, he's going to return."

"What are you getting at, Plentiful?"

"Oh, I don't know. Just that everybody else is so *for* it. Think about it. You could wind up exiled if you don't come around, and they'll just do it without you."

I withdrew and spat on the ground. "Get up."

"I'm trying to *help.*"

Taking her by the wrist I led her under starlight to Half-Moon's hut. When we got there I saw Breezy straddling my brother, her spine glistening in the dark.

"Enough," I said.

Half-Moon peered around my wife. "Enough what?"

"I know what you're doing, Half."

Breezy climbed off him and hugged her knees. Half-Moon lifted himself on his elbows, his shaping tool bobbing stiff against his navel.

"What are you talking about, brother?"

"You've initiated an exchange ceremony under false pretenses, for one thing."

"False pretenses," he said.

"To install a harassing brainwasher in my home." I dragged Plentiful to where he was. "Take back your demon and I might not consider this a breach of our brotherhood."

"Am I going back with you?" Breezy said. She turned to Half-Moon. "Are you letting me go?"

"Yes, he is," I said.

I collected her things, her headpiece and skirts, her necklaces and the fertility charms I'd carved for her that had found their way to Half-Moon's hut. Breezy followed me out the door. She was silent until about halfway home.

"You know you have to kill Rockefeller," she said.

I put my arm around her. "I know it."

Entering the hut we'd shared for eight seasons I took her shoulders in my hands. Her face was such an inspired carving of beauty and real meaning that I had to borrow from another world to express it.

"*Love,*" I said. "You are *love* to me."

Breezy stared at me in something like alarm, as though I'd confessed an ancient inner anger at her for a thing she didn't know she'd done.

For the next month my lost ancestors were silent to me, or I was in no mood to listen. Either way I got no further on the work for Rockefeller. I'd retreated from the company of my village. My belly was like a stone pulled black from a fire. Beneath my chest two cold hands pressed tightly together, and every morning I trudged to the swamp carrying the same fresh log of whitewood and a handful of tools only to find myself stymied by these hands in my chest, this smoking rock in my gut. Then, all at once, I tore furiously into the first carving.

She seemed to come from nowhere. I shaped her head, her delicate sleeping eyes. I rendered in lifelike detail the fat of her tiny legs and forearms, the flesh under her chin, the navel and folded skin of her sex, and then polished her with the tanned hide of a baby wallaby. Somehow I couldn't bring myself to show her to Breezy. It would hurt her, or maybe communicate something to her I hadn't intended, and anyway the carving wasn't hers. I had made this, with or without the aid of my lost ancestors. There's a small hut beside my house, a place for my tools and unfinished carvings, and I kept her hidden there. She was mine. When I realized this I also knew that I couldn't give her to Rockefeller.

He wasn't expected back for at least another month, but I still had nothing for him. With every failure I tried to imagine him grinning sorrowfully, looking away in sharp disappointment, but his face was a blur to me. One afternoon I took a block of striped teakwood to the swamp and waited.

Hungry and bored, I sat there as the sun rode its arc through daylight. The iron glare of the water, the breathing forest, the mud sucking between my toes, all put me in a calm, receptive mood, but I had to wonder if my heart had gone out of carving altogether. Was this how the Great Carver felt after he'd formed us from living trees at the beginning of time and then went silent forever? There were spirits moving over the lagoon, toward the sea where the dead hovered, and I looked as far as I could to find them.

"Speak to me!" I cried out. "I am alone in my life! Tell me what to do!"

At that moment, like a gift, there was a dark fleck on the water not far from where it meets the sky.

It took a long time to complete its approach. Growing bigger and more distinct, it came to the mouth of the lagoon. A man alone, swimming, made buoyant by a pair of floating metal baskets tied to his back. He called my name. It was Michael Rockefeller.

I ran into the water. Chopping through the distance between us, I could see his thin, flailing arms ahead of me, muddy and white. He wouldn't stop yelling. When I reached him he tore at my face and yanked me under. Clutching at his open shirt I managed to climb back to the air and knock him unconscious with two blows to the head.

When I finally pulled him to shore I could barely stand. In his sleep Rockefeller breathed terrifically, and I fell on the mud beside him, touching his cheek, the hard jawline through his beard. This son of an immortal king was barely a man. His face hadn't yet lost that fullness I'd carved into my secret daughter. And yet Half-Moon Terror would have him before first dark.

Rockefeller groaned. He still wore my dogtooth necklace and, in his belt, the knife he'd tried giving me at the first feast. I got to my knees to unsnap the sheath at his side and he came awake in a panic, but searching my face he seemed to relax, like Breezy after her nightmare. He said my name then, and smiled up at me in heartbreaking relief. I ripped the knife from his belt and held it to his throat. Rockefeller screamed—"Monkey fucker! I am a *monkey fucker!*" He clawed at my face, tried pressing a thumb into my eye socket, and I had to sever the cords in his arms that would permit his success in this. "Brother," I said. "You are a brother, *my* brother."

Then one more swift slice and he was quiet.

That was almost a year ago. News of Rockefeller's disappearance soon came by way of Bringing Man. He'd overloaded a dugout canoe with ancestor poles at a village somewhere east of us. A storm capsized him in the Arafura Sea, near the mouth of the Eilanden River, and according to the guide who'd clung to the overturned boat Rockefeller tried making the swim to shore. He was almost certainly dead.

"Crocodiles, probably," Half-Moon Terror said.

"Guess that settles it," I said.

"Not the way I'd hoped."

Since then Half-Moon has been elected Governor. Plentiful gave him a loud baby boy not long after, and two months ago word came down that we are now a province of Indonesia. We have a flag somewhere, and white-educated men deciding secret fates for us in Jayapura, but none of this matters. My ancestors have been appeased. They speak to me like never before, and they've even given up their anger against my Breezy.

Today I wake to the squeals of our first daughter. It's barely daylight, and this hungry voice is the sound of the sun breaking through trees, lifting the night like the lid of a basket. We have yet to agree on a name. There is only one word I can think to call her, a missionary syllable I've sworn never to harass my wife with again, so I've decided to let Breezy discover it for us. Taking the baby, she begins humming a song she made up about a charmed basket deep in the forest, just big enough for three to live in, woven to blend indistinguishably with the trees. They look so peaceful, so whole and inseparable, that I leave the two of them and strike out for my work hut.

The room is overrun with tools and noisy ghosts and half-finished carvings. Hidden safely in one corner, behind a stack of drying red logs, there waits a private vessel carved of marbled rosewood, and today my inspiration tells me to go here before getting down to work. I pull away the lid and look inside. At the bottom lies the skull of a noble, polished to a dignified shine, and next to this, my greatest creation. A child I carved to life one day, alone, under the silence of my fickle ancestry.

Their combined magic fills the room like a scent, and once again I remember where to begin.

J ACK CIRCLES THE BLOCK looking for Ann's junker Saab and tonguing his lower left canine, which is loose and clicks in his gum like a light switch. He thinks of calling to see if she's running late, but then he remembers about rethinking their boundaries, whatever that means in the middle of a divorce. In the alley he parks in a tow-away zone because he doesn't want some smart-ass valet having sex in his car (Jack was a valet in college), and because fuck it. He likes the idea of taking a cab down to the impound yard, again—everyone there looks like they just found out they're being experimented on.

Inside the restaurant, he finds Monahan sitting alone at a table for four, his hair parted and groomed the way it has been since second grade. It looks like a piece from a Lego set, a cap he snaps on in the morning and off at night. Monahan half-stands, then sits. "You're in for a treat," he says. "This guy cuts a forty-ounce porterhouse."

Jack says, "I heard that."

Monahan checks around behind Jack but doesn't ask where Ann is or if she's coming. He's the only one of their friends who doesn't become uncomfortable when Jack and Ann show up places together. People don't like divorced couples walking around in public. He says, "Sumpy's in the head."

Sumpy is Monahan's first girlfriend in twelve years. Jack's the last of their pack to meet her, though the reports have been coming in from all sides—how Monahan treats her like a child, calling her Bird or Little Sumpy. After they'd been dating less than a month, Monahan's condom broke. Of course the condom broke, Jack said: it was probably twenty years old. This was at a Padres game, top of the third. Monahan drank too much and got weepy about fatherhood. "Scared the shit out of me," he said, "but then when it turned out she wasn't pregnant, I was really in the dumps. Weird, right?" He started hugging children he didn't know and security helped him find his car. Jack stayed four more innings because he wasn't ready to go home.

At home what Jack does is sit in his empty living room in the red club chair whose mate sits in Ann's new apartment across town. He sits in the dark and watches the house across the street, which has recently been painted the color of a blueberry snow cone. He mixes drinks he doesn't drink and tries to picture how he'll react when he finds out Ann has a new lover, or a lover she'd been seeing before she left him, when the house across the street was beige. He wonders how they're going to sell their house to pay for the divorce with a ten-ton block of marzipan across the street.

Jack's first impression when Sumpy walks up is too much time in the sun, but she's cute. She has a dent in the tip of her nose and hair the color of bleached pine. Her bangs wisp into half-penny eyes that Jack imagines could be seductive in the right light. Everyone agrees she would be out of Monahan's league, except she grew up in a Christian cult, which skunked her with a strange perfume for life.

The first thing Sumpy says is, "Were you able to find kitty a home?"

It takes Jack a minute. Then he realizes she's referring to a gag email one of their friends sent around earlier that week—a picture of Jack's face and a cat's face morphed together in Photoshop. *Kitty Sad, Needs Home* the caption read. Jack wasn't sure if the guy'd recklessly forgotten or ruthlessly remembered Jack's divorce, but it creeped him out all the same. He looks at it several times a day, with his office door closed. Now he says, "That wasn't a real cat. Those were my eyes and mouth, but the ears and whiskers were, um—" He can't believe he's explaining a joke, this joke. Then he sees in Sumpy's face that she's kidding.

She says, "It fit you."

Jack takes a swig from Monahan's longneck. Sumpy says, "What I mean is, in my drawing class we learned everyone has an animal they look like and if your drawing doesn't..."

The waiter brings flatbread. It comes in a steel basket as from some futuristic dishwasher, in keeping with the over-understated decor—the unisex waiters, the light you can't tell where it's coming from. The waiter starts disassembling the fourth place setting, but Jack stops him and says they're waiting on one more. The clock behind the bar says ten after. This means Ann's stuck on the 405 in the slow lane with her blinker on to switch into an even slower lane. Monahan takes a mini bottle of Worcestershire sauce out of his pocket, an idea he got from Ann, who carries a pepper grinder in her purse.

Sumpy's art class decided her animal was a warrior horse. Monahan makes a whinnying sound and Sumpy elbows him. Jack can see horse, but not warrior horse. That's just some hippie art teacher blowing smoke up her ass. He pictures Monahan eating corn on the cob and decides his animal-double is a rat. Sumpy agrees and Monahan takes playful offense. Jack isn't sure if Sumpy knows Monahan's taking actual offense as well until she leans against him and says, "Rats are survivors."

The menu comes on a funky clipboard—one page of food, then twenty pages of wine. Jack pushes his loose tooth as far as it will go in one, then the other, side of the socket. He tries to think when he last got a full meal down. "Where's the rest of it?" he says. "There's nothing but steak."

Monahan leans into Sumpy and says, for Jack's benefit, "You see what I mean? He marries into a higher tax bracket, he forgets his roots." He almost aborts this remark midway, then goes with it anyway. "I'm talking about dead animals. I'm talking about loincloths and clubs and groaning and blood, and I'm talking about a little thing called protein."

Sumpy says, "You know, loincloths actually have an interesting history."

The waiter stops by to see if Monahan's ready for another beer and gives the Worcestershire a look. There's a ventriloquist numbness in the waiter's face, so it doesn't look like he's talking when he's talking.

Sumpy asks, like the waiter's a nurse, "Is that his second already?"

Monahan says, "You want I slow down, Sumps?"

There's a silence, then the waiter says, "To clarify. I will or will *not* fetch the Silver Bullet?"

Last night Jack bought a thirty-dollar bottle of scotch with red wax on the cap and sat in his chair picturing himself getting good and lit the way he would if a young Jack Nicholson were starring in a movie about him, but he could hardly get a glass down. In the morning the bottle and glass were still there on the table by the chair, nearly full. This was more depressing than a hangover, so he went outside and mowed the shit out of the lawn. It was six a.m. and his tooth had kept him up half the night. Every time he took a turn and saw that clown house across the street, he threw himself into the mowing with extra oomph. He mowed over a dead bird, and then he mowed under his orange tree, with mutilated orange rinds and pulp strafing his bare legs, his yard smelling like an Orange Julius.

Sumpy suggests that they order for Ann and she can eat when she gets there. Something about the way she says Ann's name, with such ease and ownership, makes Jack feel like she's plucked it from him. He can feel it in his tooth. His dentist told him the tooth was secure and to leave it alone, which was absurd, because tell him to leave it alone, that's the only thing he's sure not to do. He asks if the Caesar tastes like anchovies then says never mind and orders Ann a Cobb with no bacon and extra egg and dressing on the side, and a filet for himself.

While they're waiting on dinner Sumpy tells Jack about the day Monahan came into her shop looking for a calendar with teddy bears on it—for my niece, he said. She knew he was lying and thought the way he did it was sweet. Sumpy wants Monahan to admit he knew right away she was The One. Monahan says he wants to have a Super Bowl party. Jack wonders if he should just walk over and ask Walt to repaint his house as common courtesy. He's pretty sure Walt will resist since Jack has never done anything remotely neighborly, and in fact leaves his trash cans at the curb for days on end, against Walt's wishes.

The front door hasn't opened in so long Jack wants someone to leave just to see it move. He considers the possibility that Ann's not coming. The first night they spent in the house, Ann stopped in the middle of kissing goodnight and said how strange it was to say goodbye to someone you'd be lying next to all night, but as empty pods, and Jack said, "Yeah, we're going to sleep," and he thinks that's how he lost her, saying things like that.

Now he sorts through last night's phone call, one of those maddening conversations where Ann wants to know how he is, how he *really is,* and Jack—who just wanted to keep her on the phone, talk like in the old days—said *you really want to know?* and emailed her the picture of the mankitty, which she found troubling.

Jack was sitting in his chair, Walt's house in full bloom across the street. "You wouldn't believe what he's done with the place. We'll get twenty grand less with that thing over there."

Ann said, "I worry you're not talking to anyone about this."

"I'm serious—we'd be better off with police tape and a chalk outline on the lawn."

Ann said, "Maybe he always wanted to paint it that color, and after Marta died he finally did it."

Jack couldn't believe how painful it was to hear that. He said, "So who are *you* talking to about this?"

She was silent awhile. He thought maybe she'd fallen asleep, which she does sometimes while she's driving or waiting for prescriptions. Then she said, "I'm trying really hard to handle this right, and I don't know how that is, and if you do I wish you'd tell me." She paused. "Should I not come to dinner?"

"Come or don't come," Jack said, knowing nothing pissed Ann off more than answers like *sure* or *whatever*. But could she really not come? How could you miss seeing Monahan with a live living woman? For years the community joke was that Monahan was gay. Someone paid to have a newspaper printed with the headline *Monahan Comes Out!* above the picture of dancing multitudes on V-Day. Monahan thought this was great and tacked the clipping over his bed. On top of this, Ann's been talking about trying out The Butcher Shop for months. In the last week alone the chef's been written up in both the *Reader* and *Tribune,* one commending his respect for vegetables, the other investigating rumors that he chases his staff around with knives.

Now Monahan gets up to go to the bathroom, only instead of going down the hall with the restroom arrows he walks out the front door into the street.

Sumpy says, "Where's he going?"

"There's probably a line," Jack says.

She looks at him. "For the men's room there's a line?"

Next door there's a dive bar where Monahan's going to slam a beer. He does this. He does this even when he's out with the guys. Probably a potential Mrs. Monahan should know about this but Jack figures he's the last person to butt in on another relationship, and he's known Monahan too long, driven too many miles with the guy to too many places that didn't matter (once they drove for three hours to buy swords at a truck stop) in cars that broke down as often as not. So he takes a bite of flatbread, poppy seeds flying.

"So how are you holding up?" she asks.

He stops chewing. He wasn't expecting this, and, off-guard, he hears himself say, "It's not what I want." All of his friends think the breakup's mutual.

"Does *she* know that?" Sumpy asks.

He wants to take back what he said, start over, but it's out there. "She knows," he said.

"But have you told her?" There was a hint of frustration in her voice that surprised Jack.

"Trust me," he said, "she knows."

"Trust," Sumpy repeats, like she's checking to see if he pronounced the word right. "I always seem to find people don't know as much as you assume they do."

Jack has the feeling the conversation's gone somewhere darker and smarter without him. He wonders with a fluttering in his chest if Sumpy somehow knows Ann, and Ann's confided to her that she's changed her mind. But no, he reminds himself, he's a man in the middle of a divorce talking to a woman in love. He bends over the flatbread and, experimenting, sees how little pressure he can exert before it snaps. He says, "I hope I don't have an agenda telling you this, I don't think I do, but. He's borderline, with the drinking. He can't just slow down. He has to stop." He looks up.

She says, "Thanks for that."

He tries to think what it is about Sumpy that's bringing these things out of him, and wonders if she might agree to go and talk to Walt. Walt is at a time in life he should be thinking about salvation. Maybe Sumpy turns up on his doorstep with a bible. "Is ostentation a sin, do you know?" he says.

"Vanity is."

"Would a bright blue house qualify?"

She doesn't get a chance to answer. The waiter and another waiter come up carrying their entrées, a napkin protecting their hands from the dishes. "These are hot," the waiter says. He comes around and rotates each plate like he's setting a compass. "Don't touch these."

In the corner of his eye Jack sees the Cobb salad and Ann's silverware and napkin, still napkin origami. He sinks his knife into the center of his filet, a silky two-inch cut on the medium side of rare, but rare. He presses the loose tooth, hard, until it hurts. Ann can be forty minutes late, easy. Jack should've put off ordering but the food's here now and the best he can do is stall. He says, "This isn't rare."

The waiter says, "No?"

Jack says, "I ordered rare."

The waiter sort of bows and takes the plate. As he turns to go, Jack says, "And a glass of zinfandel to go with the Cobb."

The waiter looks at him like he's ordering this in shackles, from inside a jail cell. He says, "We're pouring Storybook by the glass."

"Perfect," Jack says.

Monahan's back splashing Worcestershire all over his meat almost before he sits down. Jack tells Sumpy go ahead and eat, don't wait for me, but she just smiles, lets her silverware lie. At the far end of the room the waiter pivots and backs into the kitchen with Jack's entrée. Through the portal on the kitchen door Jack sees him hand off the plate, then yoink his hand in the air near his throat, like he's hanging himself.

Sumpy has her purse in her lap and for some reason Jack thinks she's going to present him with a house key, but instead she hands over a laminated card. There's a picture of an empty canoe floating on a misted-over lake at dawn. The card reads *Happiness is not a state to arrive at, but a manner of traveling.* All Jack can think is that the guy riding in the canoe fell out and drowned. He turns the card over, then back. He imagines the mankitty sitting in his club chair reciting these words into his empty living room, and at the same time he realizes he's been holding the card as if Ann's been looking at it too, over his shoulder.

Then he sees the salad. Jack is on a date with a Cobb salad.

He feels warm, feverish, and he's picking up a dirty penny taste in his mouth. Without thinking, he pulls a five-dollar bill out of his wallet and hands it to Sumpy.

She stares at it. "What's that for?"

"It's for the this—" Jack holds the card between two fingers like the ace from a magic deck.

A little light goes out of Sumpy's eyes and he sees she thinks it's a joke, a cruel one. Without taking the bill, she says, "It's for you to keep. I have a lot of them." Monahan nods at this, still not talking. He's had three beers by Jack's count, which on countless occasions he's said is the worst place a person can be (*better none than three!*). Sumpy's taking time to collect herself. She does this, Jack sees, because she feels sorry for him. Ann's not coming—it's there in Sumpy's face, and it's in his face too. He can feel it. He presses his palms on the underside of the table and waits, and waits. He should explain about the card—she manages a stationery store, he thought she sold these, was selling this one—but he doesn't. He's tired of trying to make things bearable while at the same time suspecting they're not unbearable at all, but only unsafe. He wants to tell Sumpy he's not himself, that alone at home he feels like a man trapped in an elevator with a distant cousin. He talks to himself in clichés. *No sleep for the weary,* he'll say. *A man's got to eat.* When he's in an especially gory mood, he makes a point of laughing out loud while watching TV, tossing his head back, really making a scene.

Monahan's cutting his meat into dice-sized cubes like his mother does when he's at home. Not looking up he says, "I'm just gonna go ahead here."

The thought of eating makes Jack's stomach twist. Outside the sun has gone down, muddying up the windows so the reflection of the restaurant stretches out into the street, into nothingness. Tucked into the vanishing point is the reflection of the kitchen door. Jack turns and looks at the actual kitchen door on the opposite end of the restaurant. He sees a ponytail pass, then the white shoulders of someone giant. The chef, maybe. He wants to think it's the chef, the one with the temper, big bully ranging around in his cage like Walt doing god-knows-what in his blue-berry palace. Then it hits him. An idea so elegant, so smooth, Jack feels like he's thought it up with a borrowed brain. His idea is this: Walt comes out of his house once a week, to go for groceries. The rest of the time he's on lockdown, watching game shows. Walt doesn't know what color his house is. That's what's so infuriating to begin with—it's the neighbors that suffer. So late Sunday night Jack sneaks over in camouflage and paints the place with a spray gun. Just the front, just what you can see from the curb. Jack's place will sell in a week, two weeks tops. If it doesn't sell by the weekend, he sneaks over Friday night and paints it blue again for Walt's weekly run to the market. This is revelatory. Jack decides that as long as he can sit here sending meat back to the kitchen, he can figure his entire life out. Just then the waiter sets a new filet before Jack and hands him a clean knife. This time he barely opens the filet, just makes a little wound in it. "I want it to look like beef," he says, "not beef jerky."

The couple at the next table stops talking. The waiter shifts in his shoes, not sure what to do. Then he does the only thing he can, prices being what they are here, and takes the plate.

Monahan waves his knife up and down in front of Jack. "What's this," he says. *This* meaning Jack. It's a pet peeve of Jack's since forever, sending food back, harassing waitstaff, as Monahan well knows. Sumpy looks back and forth between them, uncomfortably not in on the joke, and Jack thinks how if Ann were here it'd be Monahan and Ann ganging up on him, Monahan with his little crush and Ann one of the guys.

There are fewer and fewer servers on the floor. Each time one of them flaps into the kitchen, Jack gets a look at the waiter, in the center of the gathering circle. He looks unfazed. He looks like he just let go of a bowling ball and he's watching to see what it does. Jack's never been good at thinking things through, but the fact is people like a scene and the waiter will probably get a filet out of the deal. Then someone's shouting. Pots start banging. The servers come dodging out of the kitchen, syllables and spurts of shouting spilling out after them.

A guy, possibly on tiptoe, presses his face to the portal and scans the restaurant. Then the kitchen door bucks open again and he strides out in one of those straightjacket-looking chef shirts and jeans. On the end of a serving fork, in midair, he's holding a raw steak. He's short, his hair pulled back and his eyes round, too close together, and riveted on Jack. He looks like one of those guys you think's athletic, then you toss a ball at him and it bounces off his face. The bartender shifts the blender to a higher speed then turns it off. He pours pink slush into a row of glasses. The bar customers have all turned on their stools to watch. People stop pretending not to stare.

Monahan's eyes are watery, weepy. This is where he would normally excuse himself and slip next door again, but he doesn't. For the first time in their lives Jack realizes their positions have flip-flopped, and he hopes but can't be sure their friendship didn't depend on Monahan being the comic loser, the court jester. It's a terrible thought, and worse, he suspects only Monahan knows if it's true.

The chef reaches the table, the raw filet drooping on the fork. It looks like a kidney or heart, and it makes a suction sound as he slaps it onto Ann's bread plate. He dabs his forehead on the sleeve of his nut suit and says, "Rare as I can get it, brother."

In the entire place, the only person smiling is Sumpy.

Jack looks down at the steak, the strings of blood on the white plate. When he pictures himself painting Walt's house in the middle of the night, he sees it from his bedroom window, as Ann would. He picks up his fork and Monahan's knife. Under the blade, the raw meat bulges like a fat lip, purple-red with gossamer seams. The plate skids on the tablecloth, ice tinkles in their glasses, and Ann's Cobb wobbles. At the bar, a guy slaps a bill down and says, "One bite and he yaks."

A woman two tables down in cat's-eye glasses moans when Jack forks the first bite in. He's never eaten raw meat. It's like chewing bloody chewing gum. He chews and chews and the food seems to be chewing back. He hears his jaw pop in his ears. When he swallows, the sweaty blob clogs his throat and for a minute he thinks it won't go down or up: he'll die this way, he'll get a Darwin Award. The next bite he cuts half that size. That one's like a wet little cat kiss. The still and staring restaurant fades and Jack's overcome with an underwater consciousness of himself eating in which Jack is not Jack or anything but the pure animal exertion of survival.

On his fourth bite Jack feels a *suck-pop* in his jawbone. He freezes. There's a warm streaming sensation in his gum, but if it's bleeding he can't taste it through the raw meat. He's pretty sure there went the tooth, but he's afraid to move his tongue and find out.

The chef says, "What the hell am I looking at?"

What he's looking at is Monahan's bottle of Worcestershire sauce. He's looking at Monahan's Worcestershire-drenched cubes of porterhouse, lined up in a perfect crazy row.

"You. Out."

Monahan says, "Why me? What'd *I* do?"

The chef points at the door.

Monahan looks at basically everyone, then asks, "Can I take my steak with me?"

Jack thinks how exciting it was to lose a tooth as a kid—how your parents were for some reason proud, and paid you for it—but as an adult, at this moment, he can't imagine anything lonelier. In another way it's perfect, a tiny secret uncorking, which is why instead of doing the smart thing and spitting the tooth out in his hand, he washes it down with a slug of zinfandel. This feels strangely *right* and he imagines himself swigging zin and swallowing teeth, eyes, nose, arms, until he's nothing but a stomach digesting itself.

* * *

When Ann calls, Jack's standing in the alley waiting for his cab, examining the tracks from the tow truck.

"So? How was *Meet the Monahans?*"

He can hear through the phone what she's wearing—Catholic-school skirt, clogs, that oversized jersey that says *Liberty.* He clears his throat, afraid of all the things he could say, and all the things he won't. He wants to tell her how he waited and waited, how he ordered dinner for her, but he hates feeling like she's leaving him all over again, so instead he says, "You could've come."

"I thought you told me not to." She coughs, and the cough sounds so *her* it makes him momentarily woozy. "Indulge me," she says. "I'm too sad to read and today I watched the neighbors make their dogs fuck through the fence."

"Why would they do that?"

She laughs. "I *watched* through the fence, they didn't—"

"I get it," Jack says. He backs against the brick wall, an awning of shade formed by the streetlight and building. "Let's see. There was a lot of baby talk. Possibly I insulted her."

"Oh goodie. Let's hear."

Jack feels himself smile. "I'm thinking about seeing about keeping the house."

She makes a little noise of regret.

A door opens farther down the wall and someone pushes a milk carton into the alley to keep it propped.

Ann says, "You don't sound so hot."

"I don't feel so hot." He dips his tongue in and around the naked gum. He wants to tell her about his tooth and how he's going in Monday to give his dentist hell, he wants to tell her about the card and the five-dollar bill and mowing down that pile of oranges, but he knows he has to start not telling her things or he'll never make it out of this. He'll start small, is what he'll do, and work his way up.

BEFORE SHE KILLED my brother the Polack called me out of courtesy and told me what she was going to do. I explained to her that Baron was my big brother and I loved him and asked if there was anything I could do to stop her. First she laughed—"Ha!"—then she said "Fifty grand." But I didn't have fifty grand, or even twenty grand, and my word was useless with the Polack.

I first met the Polack when she worked at Fort Worth Gold. This was before I learned the jewelry business myself and joined Baron. I was only a customer when I met her, buying a stainless-steel Cartier for an institutional client of mine. It was almost Christmas, and the sales floor stood ten deep with buyers. It was the fat time. Those were the helpful, lazy days when I made good money. It came lightly to me and I didn't resist it.

After a while I grew bored and shouldered my way to the watchcase. There was the Polack. People said the Polack took the job as a jewelry salesperson because she was the most beautiful woman in Fort Worth, Texas. She had won contests. But that was not it. She was there because there she found people all around her who didn't know any better, and she did. She was showing a big gold Rolex to an elderly black man in a black suit. I saw that she did not know how to sell. I stood next to the old man.

"I have one of those," I said to him. "See?" I pulled back my cuff to show him. I had won it two years before. Ten thousand Kirbys in one year. That's nearly thirty vacuum cleaners a day. Five million, seven hundred thousand dollars gross. It said Kirby right on the dial. Not every company can do that with a factory dial. We had a special deal with Rolex USA. "That looks good," he said to me. "You think so?" I asked her. This was the Polack I was asking about my Rolex, but neither of us knew that then. I shook the watch at her. My wrist was always too thin for a watch as big as a President. I wore Submariners too; it didn't matter to me. "Let me take the links out for you," she said. "To wear it like that is bad for the watch." "It's comfortable that way," I said. "You think it looks good?"

"It is handsome," she said. "Old," she said.

"Not old," I said. "Distinguished."

"That is what I said," she said. "Sophisticated. You listen," she said.

She wiped the Rolex she was selling with a diamond cloth. I saw the salesman next to her wince, but he didn't correct her. Dust from the diamonds would scratch the metal. Even I knew better than that.

"Try it on," I said to the man. "It helps to see it on your wrist."

She put the watch on the man. She handled the man's hand like she was fixing a broken machine.

"Do you have a mirror?" I asked her.

"Of course," she said. She went to find one. I nudged the man with my elbow as she walked away.

"Look at that. That's something."

"Not bad, huh?"

We grinned at each other. He had three gold teeth. He admired the watch on his wrist. He had thick, muscular wrists and it looked better on him than on me. The gold belonged on his dark skin. He could see himself feeding his enemies to the crocodiles in the moat behind his mansion. She returned with the mirror and angled it on its brass stand to show him the watch on his arm. There we were, together in his country. The date palms. The lions on hilltops. The hot wind in the sawgrass.

"Yes," he said. He was smiling happily. "Yes, that is the one."

You wait for that smile. You come to doubt you ever saw it. Then some customer smiles it at you and you recollect that you are not duping but helping them.

After he left the Polack found me on the showroom floor. "You sell for Rolex?" she said.

"I'm a vacuum salesman," I said. "But I'm here to buy. You want to sell another watch? Make it a big day."

"You don't look like a vacuum-cleaner man," she said. "My mother is someone who loves vacuum cleaners."

"Sensible woman," I said. "Everyone loves a good vacuum cleaner," I said. "Love is the word. But there are so many bad ones. A good vacuum cleaner you own for life. Pass it down to your grandkids. Change the belt every ten years and it will never age a day. Hardwoods, concrete, carpet. You think a Dyson will last twenty years? Cheap plastic, too many parts. You can buy one at Target. Can you buy a Rolex at Target? Manolo Blahniks? Kirby vacuum cleaners have been the world's leading professional vacuum cleaner for the home for more than half a century."

She laughed—"Ha!" That was the first time I heard that laugh, like a dog's bark. At first it disoriented you but then it made sense. And she knew when to do it. Maybe it was natural.

"I don't really sell them anymore," I said. "But I'm proud I know how. Never be ashamed of being a salesperson. It's a gift. Most people can never learn to sell. But you learn it, you can do anything. King of the practical professions, one of the few honest trades. Jesus Christ was a salesman. Mohammed. Allah. World's greatest. Paul. Those Jews. Think about Christ without Paul, huh? Ron Hubbard. Tom Cruise. So where are you from? Would you like to join me for lunch?"

"What about the watch you are buying?" she said. "You are buying today, yes?"

"That's right," I said. "Today I am a customer."

"I don't think I am a salesman," she said. "That is not a good business to be in."

I remember another time, much later. It was summer, after Baron and I had started up together and expanded the store, and the Polack was waiting outside my office. She was out on her own, hip-pocketing. For most of us hip-pocketing is like unemployment insurance, something to turn to between jobs or after bankruptcies. You pick all the cherries from the pawnshops—Swiss watches and good diamonds, antique pieces, pearl ropes, the things they pay nothing for because they don't understand real jewelry—and memo it out to the retail jewelers who need to fill up their cases. For the Polack this was regular business.

At this time, anyway, she dealt only in the big-name watches, Cartier, Rolex,

Patek, that bunch, large turn-of-the-century finished pieces, some counterfeit cut color, and loose diamonds with fake certs she was printing herself. I remember she was wearing a white dress. I had a skinny redneck in a blue baseball cap at my desk selling me a cheap four-carat diamond. It was stolen, brown, and full of carbon, and I planned to offer him a hundred a carat. Five bills tops. It would flip to IDC or Pioneer for twenty-five hundred, maybe three grand. But first I wanted to show him several diamonds of mine so that he would understand how bad his diamond was. I had prepared several stones with fake cheap prices printed boldly on the diamond papers so that he would believe you could buy pretty four-carats for a thousand or less. I had bought from this kid before and I knew he was stupid and in a hurry so I was unconcerned. But then he jumped up, yelled some word I didn't catch, and pulled a gun on me. He was bouncing on his legs and I could see that he would shoot me accidentally. So I gave him the whole diamond box. I was already thinking of the numbers I had to call: first Ken our insurance agent, then Baron at his girlfriend's, then the police, next Jude Brown our angel (they were mostly his diamonds), then Idan at IDC about his memo stones in the box, also Paul over at the bank, then my wife. But as the kid ran out of my office the Polack was there and she took him by the shoulder calmly and shot him briskly four times in the stomach. From my office it looked like she was holding him up to shoot him. But she fired so quickly you couldn't tell. Then she stepped back and the kid fell. I looked for red blood on her white dress, but she was sparkling clean. Ignoring the fallen kid she picked up the diamond box from the floor and returned it to me. "Ha!" she said. "The young!" She could not have been twenty-five years old herself at the time. She sat down at my desk and opened her briefcase. "What you got for me today?" she said, smiling. Her teeth were like silver. "Now you owe me, Martin! Ha ha! You better call the cops! The ambulances!"

The Polack had a thick Eastern European brow and greasy lips. There were hail dents on the roof and the hood of her big green Mercedes. Later she had a wine-colored convertible Cadillac. My sales manager Dennis sold her his Blancpain for fifteen hundred bucks. That was a thousand shy of what it should have been. The Polack paid less than everyone else but she always paid cash. Dennis needed the money to square up with his divorce attorney. It was a dirty divorce with a child and the worthless remnants of Dennis's old repair business in the mall. He asked me, "How can I turn this watch into cash in a hurry?" It was a beautiful automatic chronograph with a stainless head and a hobnail bezel.

"Dennis, I'd buy it if I could," I told him. "You might ask Dave. But if you're in a hurry call the Polack."

"I don't like that woman," he said.

One time the Polack and I were playing backgammon at the coffee shop behind the store and I asked her why she would never let me take her out to lunch.

"You want to fuck me, Martin?" she said. "Why don't you just say it? Say 'Hey, Polack, let's go fuck. We will have some fun!' Maybe then you could get a woman."

I thought about saying it but I couldn't.

"You don't know anything about women, Martin," she said. "They should call you Mister Dumbshit Martin. How did you get a wife?"

"I'm getting divorced," I said.

"I am not surprised," she said. "She was stupid to marry you, but she's not that dumb! Ha!"

"She doesn't want the divorce," I said.

"Marriage is not love, Martin. It is not to be a coward. Are you going to be a coward all your life? Of course you are. Mister Dumbshit Martin. Liar, thief, coward. Nice names you got! Mister Dumbshit Martin the cowardly jeweler."

For three years the Polack was my connection. Mostly I dumped to her when we were in trouble at the bank. Or if one of my salespeople screwed up and bought a drilled-and-filled diamond or a piece of antique counterfeit, I called her. And she checked our cases during the slow season like all the Texas and Louisiana hippocketers. We had a name in the Southwest for several years there. But I couldn't hang on to the Polack. My brother Baron was the personality behind the store and sooner or later everyone doing real business with us took his business to Baron. I tried not to let this bother me. You shouldn't care who put the numbers on the board so long as the numbers were up there. He was my big brother, he brought me into the business, naturally he should be better at it than me. I was a better salesman. But he found a way to put together deals that eluded me.

Those two started up together and at first it was just South American Rolexes. I ran full-page color ads in the *Star-Telegram,* ten grand a pop, and we sold a hell of a lot of watches. That was another good time. But their success together gave them exaggerated hopes. Next thing you know Baron and the Polack were bringing in counterfeit stamps, paintings, fake antiquities, you name it. You tripped over Egyptian vases on the way to the bathroom. On Black Friday, the day after Thanksgiving, movers hauled in a seventeenth-century walnut partners' desk and angled it into Baron's office. They had to tear the frame off the door. This was not a knockoff, either. It was the real thing, gigantic, bigger than a vault, two thousand pounds. You had to squeeze around the corners of the room. I don't know how Baron managed to tuck his belly under it. And there was the Polack, her back to the showroom, working deals on the phone and counting cash with my big brother. I don't think they were sleeping together. She chained a gun to her chair and kept it on the desk while she made her calls. Most of the time she was out of the store and she left the gun, so if you wanted to sit in her chair and pretend you were the Polack you had to move the gun.

I was sitting in her chair when Ronnie Popper walked in the door. He had been in prison for wire fraud and was looking for work. Ronnie Popper was the marketing genius who once owned Fort Worth Gold and Silver Exchange, where the Polack got her start. It was Ronnie who created the Rolex aftermarket. There didn't used to be one. Ronnie invented guerilla jewelry markets, which had their heyday in the eighties and now are mostly dead. After Fort Worth Gold went bust Ronnie and Baron had been partners and started our place, and it was Ronnie who talked Baron into hiring me. He taught me the business while Baron was still keeping his distance, and when the FBI came in it was Baron and me who rolled over on him and sent him to prison. I wished I could give him a job. It was a Tuesday afternoon and there I was in the Polack's chair on Baron's phone. I stood up. That was lucky because the Polack came in right behind Ronnie. The Polack pretended she didn't see him. Ronnie was nervous, I could tell.

"She works for the Feds, you know," he told me when we were back in my office. I had proudly given him a tour of the showroom. That gave the Polack some time to sidle into Baron's office and get behind that desk of theirs. "Baron should know better. Your big brother should know better."

"It was his idea," I said. "They've been putting some deals together. And I think Baron may owe her some money." I doubted that last was true but I said it nevertheless.

"They must be fucking," Ronnie said. "She's a ride and a half, I'll give her that. I remember back in the day. That office of mine. I remember one time up against the office door. That was making butter. That's what she called it, making butter. Not very romantic but she knows what she's doing. I miss that office. But I hope you're wrong, I hope it's not money. He doesn't want to owe her money," Ronnie said. "That's expensive money." He shook his head with his face down, like a tortoise. He always did that when we were in trouble. I remembered that gesture and it made me miss him.

"I wish we could put you to work, Ronnie, but I just don't have it." I felt bad. I wanted Ronnie in the store. But with the Feds following him around and Baron and the Polack pulling their shenanigans it was not practical.

"No, that's fine," he said, eyeing the Polack. "I heard she's bringing in those twelve-karat Venezuelan bracelets? Maybe I'll talk to her."

"I think she's out of the Rolex business," I lied. "Anyway do you really want to get back into Rolexes?" It was selling hundreds of fictional Rolexes over the phone and running the credit cards that they got him on. Ronnie fingered the side of his nose and grinned that old grin of his. One thing about a great salesman is those familiar, lover-like idiosyncrasies. It's difficult to fake that.

"The Anteater's bad luck but she knows money," he said.

In Houston they called her the Anteater. When inspecting packages she'd lick out the diamond melee—the tiny round-cut diamonds smaller than a tenth of a carat—while your eye was turned and store it in her cheeks like a goddamn hamster. She did the same thing with packages of diamond baguettes. She had other industry names, too. When Simons heard we were working with her he called me and told me not to do business with the Gypsy. Almost no one else dared to use that name for her.

"I've known her since she was a kid, Granddad," I reassured him. "I helped her sell her first Rolex."

There were only half a dozen jewelers in the metroplex who could call Simons Granddad, and I was one of them. I was proud of that. He called each of us Grandson.

"She's Russian mob, Grandson," Simons said. "You don't want those guys in your store."

She wore a diamond ring on every finger. You might have thought that was why a few people who hated her called her the Gypsy. But Simons called her the Gypsy because of a different story that no one liked to talk about. It wasn't because she was a gypsy, but because of something she was supposed to have done to some gypsies.

That Christmas Ronnie opened an upstairs office place in Dallas, on the second floor of an old bank on McKinney, and started shipping Rolexes all over the country. He bought the watches from Baron and the Polack, who were using the money to put together a buy of twenty jewelers working in Russia at the jewelry house that used to be Fabergé. They were actually going to purchase the jewelers from the fellow who owned them in St. Petersburg, house them in a warehouse in Arlington, Texas, and have them make counterfeit Fabergé eggs, which they were then going to sell to museums and rich Arabs and African warlords. In the meantime they weren't paying their Rolex vendors in Venezuela. Eventually the South Americans got impatient and came to town and that's when Baron came into my office.

He poured scotch from my bureau into his coffee cup. "You want some?" he asked. I started to say No, it's my scotch, but he was my brother so I said "Why not" and pushed my cup toward him. He tipped in a heavy shot.

"I have to use our line at the bank," he said. "They've got Emily."

It was the first time I had heard anyone use the Polack's real name.

"Who?"

"Come on, you know who. These fucking Venezuelans."

Personally I hate South Americans, except Argentinians and Chileans. There are no gemstones or gold that far south so they haven't been soiled by jewelry and the easy money that goes along with it. But the first time we were ever held up, at the JCK show in Vegas, it was by some Brazilians. Really it was some hookers in our hotel room who spun the safe after we passed out, but we blamed the Brazilians to everyone except the cops and our insurance agent, who had to know the truth. South Americans hit the JCK every year. They held us up with machine guns in the elevator, we said. It was straight out of *Scarface.*

"How much?" I asked him.

He took a sip of coffee. He rubbed his temple with his fist in that way he had and twisted an odd smile out at me. "Three hundred grand," he said.

"We don't have three hundred grand on that line. We'd be lucky to get a hundred."

"I know. We need to call Jude, I guess. Can you call him? I don't want to call him."

"He can't bite you through the phone."

"Can't you call him? I always call him. I don't want to call him this time. Can't you be the one to call him for once?"

He was my big brother and I trusted him. Baron was the one who had first brought our angel Jude Brown in but I called Jude this time and this time it was me who met him at the bank and signed the new papers.

We met the Venezuelans at Legends over off of Harry Hines. That was not one of our regular titty bars because it was a favorite of the Cowboys and the Rangers, so we would always run into customers. Like all celebrities professional athletes expect to pay for nothing. So we would buy their table dances and their drinks and by the end it was a thousand-dollar night instead of just two hundred each.

We weren't buying these South Americans any dances. They were three short men whose features looked like they had been cut open on their faces. Even their ears were ugly. Two of them were nervous around the topless women; they laughed and pointed rudely, and I wondered if it was their Catholic upbringing. The third sat next to the Polack with his hand on her wrist. All three wore counterfeit Men's Presidents with lousy aftermarket diamond bezels. I had the three-hundred-thousand-dollar cashier's check folded in my pocket. It occurred to me that I might stand, fake a trip to the bathroom, and depart. I could live in Portugal, Thailand, or Indonesia for ten years on that money. But I gave them the check. I showed it to the girl on my lap before handing it over so that she would be impressed and would hesitate to leave me for the rest of our evening. The Polack winked at the one holding on to her and said loudly, over the music, "You see! You see how it works! Like I tell you!" He grinned, and I realized she was taking a piece of the check. They used her to collect and she got a cut. Maybe she was using them to collect. The whole thing was complicated.

I turned to Baron. He was in the middle of a dance and he knew this woman so she let him have his hands on her ass. He had that childish, menacing grin on his face he always displayed when he was receiving a lap dance.

"We make this money back," I said. "I signed the papers. I promised Jude. We can't screw this up with the bank."

"Of course," he said. "For chrissake it's a titty bar, Clancy. Have fun."

I wasn't lying to myself. I hate that ticklish taste of self-deception. But I sincerely did not expect it when, thirty days later, Baron and the Polack did not have the green.

* * *

The bad news always happened in my office. Baron held a jeweled Thai dagger in his hands and played with it as we talked. He spun it on its tip on my desk. I frowned about the leather. He was making a hole. "What are our options?" I asked him. I moved over to his side of my desk and sat beside him like I always did when we were in trouble. I put my arm around his shoulders. This time the screwup was his fault for a change. "Cheer up. We've been in worse places," I said, generously. The Polack came in then and sat down in my chair. She picked up my phone. I thought, That is not your phone, please put it down. She had a blue vein in her wrist that stood out when she handled something. You noticed it when she louped diamonds. She was getting older but she was getting sexier, too.

"You tell him?" she asked Baron. "Ha!" she said. "What a joke!" She held the phone with her chin. She was very slender but she had a round, gentle chin. It was unexpected. It looked like a chin your mother might have. "Do not worry, little brother," she said to me, "I will get your money! Tell him, Baron! That money is for me nothing." She laughed and dialed a number on my phone.

"Do you have anybody, Clancy?" Baron asked. "What about Ralston?"

"What about Ronnie?" I said.

"Ronnie owes us almost eighty. He might surprise us. But three hundred grand is rough."

"Well, Ralston's still dangling on that consignment necklace." I had sold Tom Ralston, my best customer, a platinum Art Deco ruby-and-diamond necklace on the premise that it would wholesale for twice what he paid for it—what won't a customer believe?—and he had immediately consigned it back to me. It had sat in the case ever since with a seven-hundred-and-fifty-thousand-dollar tag hanging off it. It was worth a hundred grand, maybe. The Polack teased me about it twice a week.

"How about Fadeen?" That was Baron's crow. He was an enormously wealthy Pakistani cancer specialist in Chicago who had bought his twin daughters matching tiaras for their coming-out party. He was always good for a big diamond from Pioneer, and we reserved him for situations like this.

"Sally says they're being investigated. They've been diagnosing people who aren't sick with cancer and treating them for the insurance money. She's worried."

"Ha!" the Polack said. "Wait," she said into the phone, and tucked the receiver under her arm. "That was smart! But they catch him!"

We often solved problems by driving, so Baron and I got into his Suburban and drove out to the old Plano store. "We could ask Emily to come," he said. "She might have an idea." "This is our problem," I said.

We had closed the Plano store a year before. They still hadn't rented the space. About half the cloth wallpaper had been ripped from the sheetrock; the rest of it hung there desperately. We shot thirty bucks a yard on that fabric. There's nothing as lonely or as sweet as a dead, vacant jewelry store in a little Texas strip mall. You want to carry it in your arms to a safer place.

"Are you sleeping with the Polack?" I asked him.

"I don't think she has sex, Clancy," he said. "We're partners."

"Partners."

"You know what I mean. Of course you're my partner. She's not my partner. She's a vendor for chrissake. Anyway it's not her fault. If you want to blame someone blame me. Not to mention that you talked Jude into it. If you hadn't signed the note we wouldn't be in this mess. Now we lost the bank. It's your fault as much as mine. We need the money. Without the bank we're dead."

"Why don't we use the Ronnie solution?" I asked him. "Blame it on her, since you're not sleeping with her. It could be a theft. The way she's in and out of the store all the time. She's got a key and the codes now, right? We make some invoices for imaginary diamonds, finger the Polack for stealing them, collect the insurance, pay off the bank. Nice and clean. It's the same stunt the Calabis pulled on their in-laws. They use Ken for their insurance same as we do. And Ken went for it. He'd go for it again. Hell, maybe we could cut Ken in."

"Nice, Clancy. Good idea," he said. "Anyway you know her better than that—think what she would do to us. She's not going to roll over and go to jail. She'd take the whole thing down with her."

I wanted to tell him, This is all your fault. But keeping quiet was more satisfying. That way it was his fault and I didn't lose the advantage by rubbing it in. We barely talked on the ride home. I wanted to call my wife on Baron's cell phone but I was too shy to ask. That's how it is with big brothers. We watched the yellow grass on the side of the highway. I knew it was that familiar time again, the time when you remembered how happy you were before.

When you declare bankruptcy it is not dramatic. It's a bit like cheating on your wife. You regard the mess from a distance. First you admit to yourself that there is no money to pay the note, then you call your banker who refuses to extend you, next there is a lunch with your angel who loses his temper, and last the call to your lawyer who summarizes your choices. He explains: "If you want to hang on to the store, it's an easy Chapter Eleven." Except from your lawyer's perspective, there's no such thing as an easy bankruptcy. You want to hang on to your store, so you hide what cash you can, trim down the inventory and make a sock, warn your favorite employees, and pull the trigger.

The Polack didn't like failure so she hustled out. "It smells bad here!" she said. I helped her wrap the delicate items in gauzy paper we bought at the Container Store. She put everything in red plastic milk crates. "You see they stack, Martin!" she said. "What are you complaining about? Spilt milk! Ha!" she said. She took the partners' desk too.

I caught them one night about a month after the Polack had moved out. It was after midnight and I had left my coke up at the store so that I wouldn't go through it all but I changed my mind. There they were, the Polack shouting in Russian or Polish on top of a jeweler's bench with her hands on the back of Baron's head. You never saw how red her skin was with her clothes on. I watched them for a few minutes. She looked better naked. Naked she didn't look like she thought about money as much as I knew she did. Naked she looked trustworthy. I thought, If you sold naked, no one could outsell you. In my desk I saw they'd found my cocaine and it was all gone. Naturally Baron's was gone too. So I rifled the cash box to let him know I'd been there before they got the same idea. But probably the Polack had plenty of cash. I skipped work the next day and when Baron called at a quarter after ten I didn't answer the phone. Let him open up the store and deal with the employees if he's going to stay up all night making butter with the Polack.

I wanted to kill her then. When I came in again I sat behind my desk with my diamond tweezers pinched around my pinkie finger or on the lobe of one ear and imagined her with that tiny red laser-targeting dot following the back of her slender skull. I contemplated that for nearly a year while I explained away the bankruptcy to my panicky, childish customers. "No, new layaways are fine, it's a Chapter Eleven." "No, your diamond won't disappear while it's being set, it's a Chapter Eleven." "No, I can't cut the price any lower. No, we're not going out of business. No, it's not all cash to me now. It's a Chapter Eleven."

After the Chapter Eleven I took over. I figured all we needed was one big season.

But then Rolex USA flexed its lawyers and closed down our Rolex trade. We had to can the Christmas catalog. The last hundred grand we had I sunk into that thing. Even the trustee approved it. But those bastards knew what they were doing. They waited until days before the season started. The book was all South American counterfeit and used, reconditioned Swiss. I was debuting my new gimmick, knocking off Lexus: "Certified Pre-Owned Rolex." Rolex killed Christmas.

This was a nervous time for us. You can hide a lot while your business is running that you cannot hide once it is closed. People will wait and are careless about explanations if they think they're going to see some money out of you. When they hear that there will be no more money they become scientists and detectives, they want to see your books. At that point the best you can do is create confusion. Also you can act stupid.

By February we were converting the Chapter Eleven to a Seven, and Baron borrowed fifty grand from the Polack to pull us through the closing payroll. "We've put them through enough," he said. "I can't bounce their last paychecks." Bad idea, I said. I told him I didn't want my name near that money. "Clancy, it's a personal loan," Baron told me, but he was angry. He hinted that there was something morally wrong with me.

I took home the two bronze dogs that sat outside my office because my six-year-old admired them, and Baron took the electric MARTIN'S PRECIOUS JEWELS sign and hung it above his swimming pool. We barbecued out there a couple of times and sat in the hot tub under the green neon light. Baron planned to hip-pocket until a deal came together. Hit the pawnshops on the coast and flip diamonds and Swiss watches in the city to Dave and IDC. Suddenly we could talk the way we used to.

Between these times she called me. I remember thinking about it right after the initial meeting with creditors, while I watched everyone leave the courthouse. I was across the street, hiding in the park beneath a tree. I was hiding from the creditors, especially the customers with their consignments of their grandmothers' jewelry and their layaways for their wives' birthdays. It's a pleasant park, the only one downtown, and it has a series of forty or so short fountains arranged in a simple geometrical pattern, like a chessboard. The fountains bend when the wind blows, so it resembles a forest of very short trees made of water. The Polack had said she missed our backgammon games. I still wanted to sleep with her. Probably she wanted our customer list. I often masturbated with her in mind. There were only a hundred or so she would be interested in, but we had some good crows. Everybody in the business knew that. They knew I was the best jewelry salesman in DFW, they knew my older brother could be trusted, and they knew that somehow over the years we had accumulated the best crows.

After all the creditors were gone the Polack and I met at a Starbucks on Houston Street, not far from the courthouse and our old bank.

"I have not seen Baron," she said. She looked happy and thoughtful. "He is down here? He had the meeting with you? I see him."

"How's business?" I asked her. I didn't like her asking about Baron. "How's Ronnie?" I suspected they were fucking again. Her eyes were lidded, and I wanted to ask her if she'd been drinking. Baron said she drank before lunch. I doubt it was true. She was too cunning.

"He is old! Tell me, Martin, what am I doing with that old man? But he is smart. Smart man. You and your brother were not so smart. You were not good for me. Now no one wants to do business with the Martins. They are cheats, they say. Bad rent! That is what everyone says about you now."

"Smart enough not to go to prison."

"Ha! So you send Ronnie Popper! Again! Him first! Not me! But that time is over now. Good! No one goes to jail. I came to help you. What do you want? I am here to help you. You want money? You need something on the arm? No problem, Martin! What do you want? Just tell me! What's your plan now? You got a plan? You need help now. You know I am your friend. Old friends!"

"You said you wanted to talk to me," I said.

"I want to tell you a story. Something for you! Ha! Customers! When I was a girl, a young girl, a kid, my father took me fishing. He was a fisherman."

"I didn't know that."

"Yes, it is true. People think I am nobility but we are fishermen. He was look- ing for a fish. And he found it! He caught it. On a hook."

"That's how they catch them," I said.

"No, they use nets. You cannot make a living with hooks, Martin. You always talk like a Canadian. That's why you and Baron never make money. But when he pulled it up it was swollen. Like the baby in its belly. So he cuts it open with his knife. And what do you think was inside?"

"I don't know."

"Ha! Of course not. Guess!"

"I said I don't know."

"I know! A snake. A snake with an egg in its mouth! A duck egg!"

"I don't believe you."

"It does not matter. Why do I care if it's true? Then he cracks open the egg and what is inside the egg?"

"Another snake."

"No. Ha! That would be good. Good idea. No, something better. A diamond!"

"A diamond in the egg inside the fish."

"A duck egg! Don't forget the snake. In the snake's mouth! And then he said to me, 'You will be a jeweler.' My father called me like that. But he was right. But how did he know? Was it the diamond? No! Of course. It was because he told me. That is it. Power! Believing people, Martin. That is what I am telling you. Now you have to believe. Ha! That is not what I mean. I mean, a person you believe. Your brother. You believe him."

"You made that story up." For the first time since I originally met her, back at Fort Worth Gold, just down Houston Street from where we were sitting now, she seemed like a woman. She was lying to me to help me.

"No, it is a true story. But it is a good one. So, you help your brother."

Then I thought everything would be all right. It sounded like they were square. Maybe he had paid her back the fifty grand without telling me. But when Baron suddenly moved back to Canada I knew he was running from the Polack. I had left the jewelry business altogether and gone back to vacuums.

One morning a few minutes before a presentation I got a call in my car from Emily.

"How did you get this number?" I asked her.

"Ha!" she said. "I'm in Calgary, Martin," she said. I thought of her as Emily now that I was out of the business.

I asked her why she was calling me. She said, "You know. Ha ha!"

I explained that I didn't have any money but that I knew where to get some. This was a lie to create some room.

"You bet!" she said. "Fifty grand." I decided that Baron was already dead. That was the sort of thing the Polack could do. To prove she was cleverer than me. Or just as a joke.

I wondered what Ronnie Popper would say, or Granddad, if he were still alive. What if I called Bob and Jeremy at Pioneer, could they front me fifty grand? Or Dave? His money was always tied up in inventory but he could get liquid in a hurry if he would take the hit.

I remembered the buying trips Baron and I took together. Colombia, Thailand, Hong Kong, Israel. We had ridden elephants into the Vietnamese mountainside to buy untreated rubies and sapphires from the miners. We had slept in the same bed with the same hooker. We always planned to go with Nikhil to his cutters in Bombay but never made it.

I thought about the afternoon the Polack shot that kid outside my office. That was a happier time, I thought. You used to like my brother, I wanted to tell her. Think of all the money we made together. I almost told her about the time I saw the two of them together. I told myself I ought to hang up the phone. It was his fault. I should have fucked her.

"Let me talk to Baron," I said. "You want to buy something?" I asked her. Then I laughed. "Put Baron on the phone, Polack," I said. "That kind of money is nothing for us."

SHE HAD A RUFFLED rainbow suit—and I kissed Analiese. That's right! Underneath a roller coaster—that's right! I kissed the daughter of a millionaire. The beach swirled and roared. Her beach house had the kind of wicker that was better than leather, although my parents wouldn't believe this concept even if they heard it on Christian radio, which we listened to for seven hours in the car from Ohio. Her beach house was three sand-crusted, pavement-is-hot minutes to the actual shore, to the chipped Dumbo monorail and Pop Rocks for a dollar. It looked like a white silo. Saliva filled our mouths underneath the roller coaster like raw egg white, like pus before blood.

I said "Let's get out of here," and we ran.

The air felt like a loose slushie. At the Dairy Queen her twin brother punched me continuously right in the neck, his string body emboldened by my bewildered look. Her inner thighs wore wet sand and she downed soft white ice cream that she licked into a spike and then flattened on her taut tongue. My mind raced. I ate chocolate-dipped chocolate, my neck pounding as I swallowed, her brother's valor lodged inside it. He hung out in board shorts at the back of the line, his father's orange money tube full of Camel Lights hanging by a string around his neck.

She had the kind of intricate white body—like baby powder packed tight into a crystal vase. Her hip bones were finely cut—they shone, lotioned. Her nose tilted up. She called it, matter-of-factly, a sliding-board nose. Not knowing what I was saying, I told her I wanted to slide down it. She gave me a look. I said, "What's my nose?" She told me, by the roller coaster whose lights were dead by that hour, that there wasn't a name for it.

But I knew it was a tire swing.

I got a Pop Rock blowjob before I knew what it was. Analiese knew everything. It felt like a spangling. At night, the black waves had white ruffles, like a French maid. After she swallowed (I came) she insisted on taking a roller-coaster ride, which she said was birth control.

I told her, "You can't get pregnant from swallowing cum."

"I know," she said, "but just in case."

While upside down, she turned toward me, smiled a fine-cut smile, and tapped on her uterus, as if to say, "Look, it's working—right now!"

My parents were staying in a lit-up hot-pink vacancy-sign kind of motel a mile from the amusement and beach of Ocean City. I took her back there (her flip-flops broke from the walk) while my parents were out gambling. We swam in the cracked pool and it turned her blond hair green. She took a shower while I sat on the bed. She was stressed about her hair.

She said, "Where's your mom's shampoo?"

I said, "She just uses what they give you."

"You know they dilute that times a thousand," she said.

I opened the bathroom door. "I can't hear you," I lied.

"They dilute it times a thousand," she sang, mocking all singers in all showers everywhere.

"Where's your bathing suit?" I said. I looked around the bathroom for it. Before I could find it, she flung aside the shower curtain and stood there, dripping and soapy, bubbles disorganized, all over her, still wearing it. Ruffles. I had no idea why.

I didn't know I was dangerous.

"I'm going to use the rest of this," she said. "Because they dilute it times a thousand."

We poured pixie sticks into a bag of coke we found in a pair of my dad's dress socks.

"Argyle," she told me.

We found condoms, said they were balloons for retards with gigantus of the mouth. We ate a gram of pot and half a bag of cherry Fun Dip. I licked a Fun Dip stick and drew my invisible name on her stomach with it. She dared me to put a red Warhead up to my bare eyeball. I called the hotel desk and asked them if they had any tape for a broken flip-flop. They said maybe if we came to the office they'd have some for us. When we got to the office, no one was there. There was a computer printout taped to the counter that read NO EXTRA TOILETRY REQUESTS. We rang the desk bell. We stole the desk bell. We threw it off the top of the Ferris wheel. We leaned down upon the wind and tried to listen for the ding of it coming down on a head. We bought new flip-flops with her dad's cash, crisp from recent blackjack, all twenties. She bought me a shirt that said "I'm the Boss So Do What I Say" in letters that jumped blue. I had a rat tail.

"The only slot machine my dad plays is an ATM," she said, an obvious quote from the man himself. We were on her porch, with her brother. They insisted together that it was the front porch, even though it was in the back of the house.

"This defies all logic," I said.

They said, "But this door goes to the living room and that door [they pointed around the white silo, their arms arced] to the kitchen."

"But this porch is behind your house!" I screamed, which, as though my throat were rigged to the rich, clicked on a light on the top floor.

We had different philosophies. They determined the front and back of a house by the order of the rooms inside of it. A kitchen door is always a back door was their school of thought. I determined it the same way I'd determine that the dark side of the moon is the back and the bright side is the front—no matter where the kitchen was inside of it. I just didn't care about the rooms inside of the moon. It threw the waves toward us with the kind of salt that bruised you.

We snorted pink-lemonade powder in her parents' kitchen while her parents were dining at the Taj in one of the onions. Her twin brother, who drifted in and out of the kitchen, apathetic in an interested sort of way, said he wouldn't snort pink-lemonade powder unless I snorted the contents of a Camel Light. I did it, no problem. We told him about putting the Warhead on my eye, how I cried out of it so much that we collected my tears in a miniature bathroom cup and I made her drink it.

"Where was this?" he asked, and we both fell silent, as though we'd been somewhere he wouldn't want to know about.

"His parents' motel," she finally uttered. From the downstairs, you could see all the way up to the top of the silo. Metal stairs wound around its edges, leading to the bedrooms, which had frosted-glass-brick walls. The house used space weird, and I stared up into it, trying to figure it out, architecturally.

He looked at my shirt. He said, "Whatever. You're the boss."

We put the pink powder on a paper towel and, defying all gravity, it went up her sliding board. I took it through both nostrils. Her brother smoked a cigarette, exhaling into an empty liter of Coke he'd developed for this purpose. My nose started to burn, even on the outside, and to comfort it I buried it entirely into the white plush carpet in the living room. The living room was a silo circle. She sat on my back and sang a Quaker camp song. Her brother inserted his cigarette in the bottle and started singing it, too.

My nose started to bleed. We spent the entire evening dumping combinations on top of the red spot on the white carpet, trying with all our tormented might to get rid of it. We used combinations of bleach, dish soap, bar soap, vinegar, boiled water, all of our spit, club soda, Drano, rubbing alcohol, Clinique foundation, Windex, clear Chap Stick, SSS, eyedrops, SPF 30, calamine lotion, her parents' lube which came in a zigzag bottle, ice, Alka-Seltzer, contact fluid, nasal decongestant, Vagisil, Fantastik, Sun-In and a flashlight, nail-polish remover, detergent, Oxy pads, and vodka on a cotton ball. My blood spot turned pink, then beige, Tide blue for a while, and then into thick violet snot.

We waited around for it to dry and then we'd try to peel it off. I stared at her. We agreed to wait an hour and then we'd see. It was the hour of doom. Her ruffles didn't move. If we could get it off the carpet, we'd be friends forever, and we'd lose our virginity to each other that night, the roller coaster roaring and the people screaming and my cock would click on like a light, the soul that had been hovering over it all my life would enter it, and live there until I died. If we couldn't—

I started high school and smoked Marlboros against brick walls for a year. I grew bangs. I went to Ocean City the next summer, 1990, and asked at her parents' home if Analiese was around. Or her brother. I walked around the silo into their backyard to what I remember was considered the front door—a nice touch. But when her father opened it to see who it was, he looked perplexed about why I should choose this door when it was so clearly in back of the house—a door you'd have to trespass to knock on. I felt like a miscreant. He looked at me like I was one. He was the emperor inside the moon and I was knocking on its dark side. I could see just an inch from his hip a slim telephone table that seemed awkwardly placed, a little too central for its outward purpose, the telephone cord buried completely into the plush of the carpet I knew too well.

Once dried, my blood turned back to red, although deeper, and thick like dried tar. Analiese cried. I thought of trying her tears on it—a last, magical resort, the moral to the story—but I hesitated, and then her brother said I had to leave. Whatever. I wasn't the boss. He guessed. I lit a lighter behind my head and burned my rat tail off, wet it in a white ruffle of water and left it coiled atop an abandoned sandcastle.

Her father told me she'd gone to the beach. I'd find her and her brother both at the beach. It's impossible to find somebody at the beach, so fuck you. I sat smoking a Marlboro, contemplating the army, and death without love. I thought about getting a tattoo and found a place off the boardwalk that wouldn't card me. I had a man write *Analiese* across my collarbones, as if hung there like a black HAPPY BIRTHDAY in a doorway. I did it as a protective measure. It was the only way to truly prevent myself from going to her house again (and again)—because it would just be too bizarre for her to see me a year later with her name hung permanently up on me. I knew I'd obsess over it, would have to go back to the white silo. I would rush roughly toward it. I'd want to see my blood again beneath the telephone table. I'd knock down her father with new high-school muscles and knock down the telephone table. I'd stand over that red spot again. I'd stare down at my heart from a great distance, from outer space.

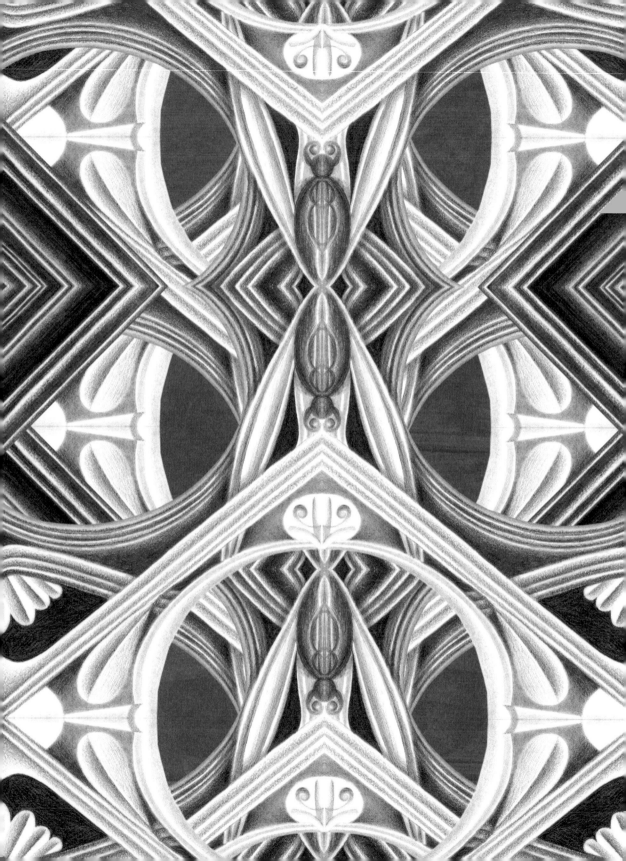

CONTRIBUTORS

CHRIS BACHELDER is the author of the novels *U.S.!, Bear v. Shark,* and *Lessons in Virtual Tour Photography* (an e-book available free at mcsweeneys.net). He teaches in the MFA program at the University of Massachusetts in Amherst.

ANN BEATTIE is the Edgar Allan Poe Professor of English and Creative Writing at the University of Virginia. She has no hobbies.

CAREN BEILIN'S fiction has appeared in *Zembla Magazine, Quarterly West,* and can be read online at www.3AmMagazine.com. An essay on how she writes next to a picture of her apartment's water heater will appear in an upcoming book called *How I Write.* She lives in Philadelphia.

RODDY DOYLE'S new novel, *Paula Spencer,* was published in January. A collection of stories, *The Deportees,* will be published in early 2008.

CLANCY MARTIN is a former jewelry salesman and store owner who now teaches philosophy at the University of Missouri in Kansas City. His stories, essays, and translations have appeared in *NOON, Parakeet, Philosophy and Literature,* Barnes and Noble Classics, and elsewhere. His new translation of Nietzsche's *Beyond Good and Evil* will appear in 2007. "How to Sell" is drawn from a novel about the jewelry business that he is presently completing.

CHRISTOPHER STOKES is the author of dozens of unpublished stories. He lives in Oxford, Mississippi, where he is currently wrapping up his MFA at Ole Miss and finishing his first novel.

WELLS TOWER writes fiction and nonfiction. He lives in North Carolina.

DEB OLIN UNFERTH'S fiction has appeared in *Harper's, Conjunctions, Fence, NOON,* the Pushcart Prize anthologies, and other publications. Her first book is forthcoming from McSweeney's.

SHAWN VESTAL is a long-time newspaper reporter and editor who lives in Spokane, Washington. He's a student in the MFA program at Eastern Washington University.

APRIL WILDER is currently the James McCreight fiction fellow at the Wisconsin Institute for Creative Writing. She has recently published stories in *Southwest Review* and *PRISM International.* She is working on a book of short stories and a novel, *I Think About You All The Time, Starting Tomorrow.*

—IF YOU STOLE THIS ISSUE OF MCSWEENEY'S—
THERE IS A SAFER AND MORE LAWFUL WAY.

As a subscriber, you'll get four issues for just $55, a substantial savings off the fluctuating cover price. The stories will always be good, but in other aspects almost every issue will be notably different from the ones that came before it. This one, Issue 23, comes wrapped in a very large jacket, but Issue 24 might be delivered in gaseous form. Probably not. But we thought about it, and that alone says something. Also, new subscribers receive a free copy of *The Better of McSweeney's,* an anthology of letters and excellent stories from our first ten issues.

THERE ARE ALSO THESE THINGS FROM THE SAME OFFICE IN SAN FRANCISCO'S MISSION DISTRICT

THE BELIEVER

Our colorful monthly magazine of expansive writing covers art, music, books, philosophy, and ninjas, and also includes monthly columns by Nick Hornby and Amy Sedaris. It's all illustrated by Charles Burns and Tony Millionaire, and you'll save a good percentage off the $8 cover price by subscribing—it's only $45 for ten issues. And when you subscribe, you'll also receive an enormous poster featuring over a hundred of Burns's astonishing portraits.

WHOLPHIN

A quarterly DVD magazine full of rare and unforgettable short films. Every issue includes explosive documentaries, incredible foreign animation, otherwise-unreleasable American comedies, and many things you've never seen before. Just $40 for a year.

THE McSWEENEY'S BOOK RELEASE CLUB

BRC subscribers will receive our next ten books, roughly one a month. Novels, art things, whatever. We'll send them all for just $100. It's a very good deal.

FOR ALL THIS AND MORE (NOVELS, T-SHIRTS, BACK ISSUES) THERE'S
—STORE.MCSWEENEYS.NET—